THE HAND OF KARMA

by

Haimes Hensley

Published by Haimes Hensley

ISBN: 978-1480009608

Electronic Adaptation provided by Stunning Books

For Mom. We miss you.

ACKNOWLEDGMENTS

To our Mother, she called us her 'lima beans' and believed in us from the start. The greatest thing she ever did besides making us sisters was to teach us the importance of love, laughter, and kindness. Wish you were here.

And to Diane Marcou, our teacher, your encouragement was more valuable than words can express. You always made us feel like your star students. You called yourself a 'bawdy old hippie' but to us you were a one-of-a-kind inspiration.

We are eternally grateful to the nurses and patients at Morton Plant Hospital, Clearwater, Florida, who listened with eagerness as we worked on our manuscript while NanC was undergoing chemotherapy treatments.

And last, but certainly not least, to our family and friends who sometimes felt neglected, thank you for giving us the freedom to pursue our passion.

CHAPTER ONE

Pinellas County, Florida

The rain had turned into a drizzle which did nothing to lift the oppressive humidity that was unusual this early in the year. Cursing under his breath, the man in a black Toyota wiped the sweat from his forehead. "No A/C. Not tonight," he said aloud. He couldn't take a chance on drawing attention to his parked car.

He closed his eyes and without a conscious thought he rubbed the shaft of the tire iron cradled between his legs. "No, Daddy," he whispered, "no, don't." He shuddered as the memories came back.

A couple walked by. He let the metal tool slip to the floor and tugged at his baseball cap pulling it down over his eyes. He remained motionless until they passed.

Across the street the lights at the sports bar turned off. The front door shut when the last customer exited.

He read the note once more, folded it with a sharp crease and tucked it into his shirt pocket.

The waiting man saw his prey. "Your time has come, Lenny Chambers."

Lenny Chambers was a handsome man with a swagger of confidence and the sway of someone who had too much to drink. Lenny stumbled up next to the black car, leaned against the back fender and puked into the grass. He took a few steps and stopped. He fumbled to light a cigarette then staggered toward his pickup truck parked under the overpass in the remote parking lot of Tropicana Field.

The man inside the car scanned his surroundings—saw no one else. He left the Toyota, tire iron in hand, and overtook his victim.

The inebriated man had no time to react when the tire iron smashed into his knees, popping them like an aluminum bat bashing a baseball.

Before Lenny could scream, the attacker swung again.

Lenny raised his arm to shield his face. The weapon broke his forearm. Another strike cracked Lenny's other arm. The final blow came down across his head. He lay crumpled and bleeding—his mouth agape.

The assailant reached into his shirt pocket and fished out a rag from a plastic bag and shoved it into the helpless man's open mouth. Lenny's eyes bulged as he choked on gasoline fumes, desperate to get air into his lungs.

The attacker opened his lighter and knelt down to ignite the rag, making sure he made eye contact with Lenny. The cloth burst into flames.

Lenny's face lit up in the darkened night. He shook his head in a frenzy trying to dislodge the inferno in his mouth but only succeeded in waving the rag back and forth like a distress signal.

The man turned from his victim and pulled a small pouch from the pocket of his jeans. He tossed the pouch next to Lenny's charred face.

"Karma, brother," he said, "Karma."

CHAPTER TWO

Stretched out on the bed, he stared at the ceiling fan listening to the hypnotic click of the motor. He now knew what contentment felt like. The nagging depression that had haunted him for so long was gone! He climbed out of bed and stepped over his bloody, mud-soaked clothes and shoes that were piled on the floor. The thought of last night comforted him. This would be a good day.

He rubbed his forearms scarred from years of cutting and shivered when a blast of cool air hit his naked body.

He walked to the antique desk and opened his journal. 'Karma' was written at the top of the page in Peacock Blue ink.

With the fountain pen that once belonged to his father, he began to write:

> *Mom and Dad,*
> *Today I am free of my Karma just as she predicted. I'll turn forty soon and will have peace for the rest of my life.*
> *Thank you for giving me the strength to rid the earth of one more unfit human being and giving his family a chance at life. I hope the three of you rot in Hell.*
>
> *He signed it: Your Devoted Son*

"I'm starving," he mumbled and checked his watch. There was plenty of time to dispose of his bloody shoes and clothes, shower, get dressed, and go to the Pancake House for breakfast before his twelve-thirty meeting.

He'd finished taking care of the mess in the house and went into the garage. He thought about the tire iron in the trunk of the car. He'd have to clean it later.

He removed the gray dust cover from his other car; his fun car, his silver Jaguar convertible. He bought it when she told him he deserved to do something nice for himself. The odometer read fourteen thousand nine hundred and fifty-one miles.

"I'll put more on it now," he said aloud. "I deserve it. I've earned it." He pulled out of the driveway and onto the street. "Good morning star shine," he sang, "the Earth says hello . . ."

#

It was a perfect spring day in Clearwater. The sun was bright and in the air was a slight breeze off the Gulf of Mexico. The forecast predicted temperatures in the low eighties.

She opened her office windows to let in the fresh air. At the nearby mirror, she stopped to admire her new coif. She was pleased that she could pass as a natural redhead. She leaned in closer. "Oh, brilliant!" The blonde roots were showing already. "Time for a touch up." After giving her hair one more fluff, she answered the incessant knocking at her door.

"This was too big to put in your mailbox. There's no return address and there's thirty-seven cents due on postage."

She paid the mail carrier, and with package in hand, sat at her desk. Inside the padded envelope was a card:

My Dear Friend,

Of all the psychics I've been to, you're the only one who predicted my book of poems would be published. So, I'm sending you my first autographed copy.

Warm Regards, Your newly famous client, Nicole Angelo

She smirked at the title, <u>KNOWING</u>. "How trite." She scanned the sophomoric rhymes throughout the book and snickered. "Like I want a book of bad poetry and for this I paid postage!"

She tossed the book into a drawer and closed it as her twelve-thirty client arrived.

At the conclusion of his reading, she said in her proper British accent, "It's been delightful."

"Wait! Isn't there more you want to tell me?" he implored. "You sure you haven't left anything out?"

"I've covered what we need to discuss today," the psychic replied. "I'm sure I've told you all that was necessary."

"Don't you see anything about last night? I did what you—"

"STOP!" she snapped. "There's no need to discuss that issue." She leaned forward. "Suffice it to say you're on the right track. Do keep up the good work." She stood without further remark and started toward the door.

He tapped his watch. "Our time's not up yet. I have half an hour left!"

Her brow furrowed and she returned to her chair, then jotted a reminder for herself—tell clients scheduled times are UP TO an hour.

He spoke first. "I had to tell you . . . when we met you said that my karmic debt would be paid in my forties—that I'd find peace and happiness. Well, you know I'll be forty next week and when I woke this morning, I knew it had already started!"

"How grand for you." She glanced at the clock on her desk.

"I hope you know I didn't say that so you would remember my birthday."

"Oh. But, I did. I could never forget your birthday!" She reached into the desk drawer. "Truth be told, I bought this especially for you, but I was waiting for next week to post it to you. If you don't mind that it is not wrapped, I will give it to you now."

"I can't believe it! You did remember!" He opened the poetry book. "It's autographed! I never expected a gift. I don't know what to say." With outstretched arms, he leaned over to give her a hug, but she pushed her chair back away from him.

"Just have a happy birthday, and I do hope you find this book as meaningful as I did. Now, if you will excuse me," she said, "I am expecting an overseas call," and ushered him to the door.

#

Unable to contain his eagerness, he opened the book as soon as he got in his car. <u>KNOWING</u>. The perfect title. "She actually remembered my birthday! This is the first time since I was eighteen that anyone remembered!" He leafed through the pages. There it was, right in front of him—a poem entitled, 'Sharing Our Secrets.'

> *Mine to give, yours to keep,*
> *Only the two of us know.*
> *That special place between two souls,*
> *Where only we can go.*

She read this same poem. That's why she bought the book 'especially' for me! This is my sign.

As soon as he arrived home, he poured himself a drink then stripped off his clothes, a ritual he began years ago. He couldn't remember when exactly or why he started the habit, but he liked the feeling of nakedness. He plopped on the bed, picked up his special birthday gift, and began to read. Each poem held a different meaning for him. He dozed off remembering her words, 'I bought this especially for you.'

#

He switched on the television news as soon as he woke. Still naked, he went to the kitchen to microwave his dinner. His attention was diverted to something the news anchor was reporting. He dashed into the living room and turned up the volume. On the screen was a picture of the Tropicana Baseball Dome. A reporter was describing the grisly find near the remote parking lot . . . "that of an unidentified body. Police are giving little information except to say it appears to be a homicide."

"NOT A HOMICIDE, YOU IMBECILE!" he shouted at the television. "THE BALANCE OF JUSTICE!"

The report reminded him of the bloody tire iron in the trunk of the Toyota. After he ate, he went to the garage to clean the Karmic tool and returned it to its compartment. *Nothing suspicious about a tire iron in a trunk.* Pity no one will ever know the sacred significance of this simple tool. No one, that is, except Lenny Chambers.

CHAPTER THREE

Los Angeles County, California

Christina Dominguez pulled into a parking space, almost side-swiping the car next to her. She rushed into the building and waited at the elevator pushing the call button again and again. The elevator stopped at the seventh floor. Christina hurried to the office of Allison Rogers.

"Come in, Christina." Allison greeted her with a smile. "It's good to see you again." Christina was so much thinner than at her visit six months ago . . . her eyelids swollen and red from crying. That natural beauty with perfect posture had morphed into a stoop-shouldered old woman.

"I know how busy you are, Allison. Thank you for seeing me so quickly. I don't know how I'd cope without your psychic readings."

Allison shook her hand and felt Christina's ice cold fingers then went to the thermostat to turn off the air conditioner.

"I don't know where else to turn." Christina cried. "My husband did it again! But when I questioned him, he pushed me and called me a crazy, jealous woman. Carlos says I'm the only one he loves, but if he loves me, why does he keep doing this to me? Will he ever stop?"

"We have talked about this before, Christina. You keep asking

THE HAND OF KARMA

the same questions and I keep giving you the same answers." After all these years, it was still hard for Allison to understand why people would come to her for psychic help then ignore her advice. "No Christina, I don't see him stopping."

The distraught woman leaned forward. "How can you be sure that what you're seeing is true? Could you be wrong? Do you think that's possible?"

"Christina, it is possible. However, every time I have seen this in the past, you have confronted Carlos just to find out what I told you was true."

Exasperated, Allison drew in a breath. "I know what you want me to say, but I will not tell you something just to make you feel better. Besides, would you really want me to do that?"

"Please, just tell me what to do! I need direction."

"I cannot tell you what to do, I can only tell you what the situation is. It is your life. You have to make your own choices." Allison saw the desperation in Christina's eyes but would not cross the line in deciding another person's fate. "As much as I would like to help, I cannot do it for you. I do not walk in your shoes."

They sat in silence while she gave Christina time to pull herself together.

"I don't mean to be difficult," Christina apologized.

"I understand, Christina."

Christina reached across the desk for a tissue and inadvertently knocked over a picture. "I'm sorry. I'm so clumsy." She reached over and set the frame upright. "Is that your husband with you?"

"Yes, that's my husband, Kent."

"He's very handsome, and your hair was much blonder then. Where was this taken?"

Allison said the photo was taken in Maui last year, a romantic trip from her husband. She picked up the spark of unintended envy that the tearful Christina felt.

"Allison, you can't possibly imagine what it feels like to have someone you love so much be unfaithful."

If you only knew! Kent planned the trip to Maui to make up for his latest infidelity. He swore he would never be unfaithful again . . . she hoped Kent meant it this time. She loved him, but there'd be no more chances.

"Christina, I think I've helped you as much as I can. I have recommended a marriage counselor several times." Again, tears overflowed from her client's eyes. Allison knew that suggestion failed.

"My husband is a proud man. I brought it up and Carlos became so furious he stormed out of the house and didn't come home until two in the morning, very drunk! He didn't talk to me for days!"

"If Carlos is not willing, there is nothing more I can do. If he refuses to meet with a counselor, maybe you should talk to an attorney or seek a therapist for yourself."

"We're Catholic!" Her hand went to the crucifix she wore at her neck. "Divorce is out of the question, isn't it?" Allison knew the question was rhetorical. "I can forgive him for what he's done if you can tell me he's going to stop seeing other women."

"I am sorry I cannot say that because that is not what I see!" It distressed her to have to be so blunt.

The woman sucked in her breath as if she had just been kicked in the solar plexus.

"Christina," Allison handed her another tissue and the cassette recording of her reading. "Please take my suggestion to seek legal counsel, or at the very least, hire a private investigator."

She had such empathy for Christina Dominguez. Allison knew the pain of betrayal, but felt it was necessary to tell her the truth about Carlos' behavior.

Thankful the work day was done Allison walked to the window to clear her mind but couldn't rid the negative energy that blanketed the office. As a general rule, Allison didn't have difficulty disconnecting from the people she read. This time was different. There was something ominous she could not see, but felt. A sudden flash came to Allison. Christina would be a young widow.

#

Relaxed after her four-day weekend with Kent at their cabin on Lake Tahoe and ready for a full schedule of work, Allison arrived early to her office. She opened the door and froze in disbelief at the bold red words painted on the back wall: U R NEXT BITCH.

Stunned and unnerved, she stepped over the broken glass, books thrown about, and stuffing from the ripped sofa, all the while surveying the room as she dialed 9-1-1. What most disturbed her was pieces of the heirloom vase Mother had given her on her wedding day strewn across the floor. A jagged piece lay at her feet.

She dialed Kent's number. "It's me. Call me right way. It's important."

By the time the police arrived, she had stopped crying but now was mad as hell. "Officer Russell, I can't believe this happened to me!"

"Ma'am, I can't believe you entered the office before we arrived. That was dangerous. Can you tell me what's missing?"

"I'm not sure of anything being stolen, just vandalized." Shaken, she looked around and took in the violent destruction again. She had no idea who would do this to her or why. Then she remembered. "Every now and then, there would be a hang-up call or a voice mail from someone accusing me of being in league with the devil or being a false prophet. But, I never take it seriously."

"The sign on your door says 'Consultant.' He raised an eyebrow. "What exactly is it that you do, Mrs. Rogers?"

"I'm a psychic consultant."

"Uh huh." His note taking continued. "Why didn't you contact us when these calls started?"

"They weren't threatening. I thought they were just from some nut letting off steam. Nothing ever came from the calls."

"Mrs. Rogers, are you sure you can't think of someone who

would have done this?"

"Officer Russell, it could have been anyone," her frustration mounted. "I suppose it could be one of my clients or someone they know."

"So, what makes you think that? Why would one of them leave you this warning?"

She rubbed her forehead, sighed and started over. "I read for a person once or twice a year and always tape record the sessions. I give them the tape so they can refer to it as needed. Maybe someone got hold of a tape that shouldn't have."

"And why would that be a problem?"

"Officer, I tell my clients everything that comes to me. I see very personal details and sometimes it includes infidelities or even unethical activities."

"What do you mean, see? What's that mean?"

"It means I am psychic, officer! You know, clairvoyant. It means I see things others do not." She could have been talking to her elbow for all the sense it made to him.

"Let me get this straight! Without evidence, you tell people their spouses are cheating, their employees are stealing, or God knows what else, and you're shocked when something like this happens?"

"You're saying this is my fault?"

"Mrs. Rogers seems to me you are responsible. Where do you get off accusing people like that without proof?"

"Proof? You mean like proving the extra-curricular relationship you have with your daughter's basketball coach?"

"STOP RIGHT THERE!"

A deputy dusting for fingerprints turned in the direction of the commotion. "Hey, Russell, everything okay?" he called from across the room.

"Just get back to work!"

Russell glared at Allison. Spittle formed in the corner of his mouth. He leaned in and spoke in a monotone. "Watch your mouth, lady."

He called to the fingerprint specialist, "I'm done here," then left Allison standing in the middle of the room. At the door, he turned to face her. "Oh, Mrs. Rogers," he bellowed, "if you're a psychic, how come you don't know who did this?" He left without waiting for an answer.

The deputy finished checking for prints, adding fine black dust to the mix. As soon as the officer left, she picked up her appointment book from her desk, reviewed the damage one last time, and closed the door behind her. She would cancel her work for the rest of the week when she got home.

Allison dialed Kent's cell, again. Then, she called the house. Irritated that he hadn't returned her calls, she hoped he'd be home when she arrived.

Allison turned her car onto the driveway, still shaken from the day's events. Aggravated, she walked past Kent's Porsche but didn't know the cream-colored car parked behind it.

Inside, she dropped her purse and car keys on the foyer table. "Kent? I'm home. Where are you?" She climbed the stairs and called out toward the study. "Kent? Why didn't you call me? You're not going to believe what happened!"

In the master bedroom, she kicked off her shoes then returned downstairs and remembered the strange car in the driveway. A sinking feeling hit her. "Oh, Kent. Not after your promise!" She rushed through the downstairs and not finding anyone, went out to the pool.

She followed the flagstone pathway to the guest house. Voices came from inside. Allison opened the door. It took a second for her mind to adjust to what she saw. There before her stood Kent in all his naked glory. He yanked the afghan that was draped over the sofa and tried to shield his lover from her.

"NO! You BASTARD!"

"Allison, it's not what it looks like. Let me explain!"

"You are wrong, Kent. It is exactly what it looks like. I hope you and Fernando will be very happy together!"

CHAPTER FOUR

Pinellas County, Florida

News articles littered the kitchen table. He scrutinized all of them, reading and re-reading each one to ingrain the story in his mind.

Aaron Johnson, Jr., three years old, dead. Locked inside a closet with a box of cereal and juice. Son left with babysitter so father could go fishing. No babysitter could be located. Mother in jail. Aaron Johnson, Sr. the sole guardian.

"Aaron, there's a special place in hell for your daddy," he spoke to the photos in the papers. "And I'm going to send him there."

He rummaged through his work bag, making sure he hadn't overlooked any of his usual tools. They were all there: knife, plastic bags, duct tape, tire iron, vinyl tarp, rope, and rags. Today he bought some specialty items—fishing line, and a crab trap he tossed in the trunk. He'd reserve those for his moments of inspiration.

He read the note once more. The instructions were clear and he would never want to disappoint. Besides, he was doing this for himself. Good Karma would free him.

He had time to dress before he met the fisherman. Timing was everything in these matters. Every element had been planned and alternate strategies worked through in the event of an unexpected variation of the father's routine.

A news bulletin on the kitchen television caught his attention. "Aaron Johnson, Sr. was found dead on his driveway from multiple stab wounds. Neighbors reported no unusual sounds or strangers in the area at the time of the attack. The victim is the father of three-year-old Aaron Johnson, Jr. who was discovered dead in his bedroom closet a week ago."

"FUCK!" He slammed his fist on the tabletop. "He was mine!" he spat, then calmed himself. "It's okay," he said to the picture of the little boy, "the bastard's burning in hell now. I'll earn my good Karma points on the next one."

He picked up each clipping with deliberate care, creased them in half, and put them all in his project folder along with the note.

CHAPTER FIVE

Los Angeles County, California

Allison had trouble sleeping so at six-thirty in the morning, she decided to drive to the marina and take a walk. She thought about the words painted on her office wall.

"Who cares if I am next?"

She gazed at a distant cruise ship on the horizon. No tears would come. Some pain hurts too much to cry. The emotional turmoil she faced was taking its toll.

Her mother used to call her the 'Eternal Optimist.' She always saw the best in people and in life. Now that optimism was challenged.

She sat on a bench and thought back to when she'd met Kent; handsome, strong, and a major league baseball player! He'd just signed his contract with the team and was celebrating with his buddies at the Polo Lounge. She was there with Lancie and Paulette. He bought her a drink. They talked for hours, and three months later they were married in Las Vegas at the Little Chapel.

They were happy. She saw clients when Kent was on the road with the team and only went to work two days a week when it was off-season so she could spend all of her free time with him.

After they bought their house in Brentwood, their life seemed picture perfect. She knew Kent loved her with as much passion as she loved him, but she also knew if she examined his love closely, she'd find a flaw.

Allison had the same feeling she'd had as a child when she knew her father was going to leave. She pretended everything was fine and if she didn't look too hard, it wouldn't happen. She had the knack to compartmentalize the bad and focus on the good.

"Allison. Allison Rogers!"

Startled, she jerked around. "Yes?" No one was there. She waited.

Two squirrels scampering up a nearby eucalyptus tree distracted her. The chattering duo disappeared into the heavy foliage.

"Allison. Allison Rogers!"

She whipped around.

There was no one in sight. She knew what she heard and it wasn't her imagination! "I'm stressed, but I'm not crazy!" Filled with mounting angst, she gathered her things and jogged to her car.

She opened the driver's door. Again, the disembodied voice. "Allison. Allison Rogers!"

Wary now, she locked the doors and scanned the area around the marina. Everything appeared normal. Unsettled by the unknown person calling to her, she took off.

#

Allison saw Kent in her attorney Barry Glenn's office and found it more difficult than she imagined it would be. She shook Barry's hand after the depositions were over and left the office. Kent stayed behind with his lawyer. Allison was glad their paths wouldn't cross outside.

She got into her vehicle and headed for the interstate, entering the on-ramp of the I-10. After a minute, all cars came to an abrupt halt. Rush hour in Los Angeles was bad, but now an accident? She just wanted to get home.

After ten minutes of no progress she turned on the radio to a classical station to help her unwind. The red warning light on the gas gauge flashed. Empty.

"Impossible! I cannot be out of gas. I filled up this morning!" She rested her head in her hands. "Crap!"

A loud horn blast alerted her that traffic had moved. She pulled away, took the nearest exit, and drove to the first gas station she saw.

The gauge must be broken, she thought, it must be.

She swiped her credit card and readied the nozzle. The pump stopped at twenty gallons. After she replaced the nozzle, she bent to check under the car for a leak.

"How can this be?" The ground beneath was dry. Movement at the rear of the car! Men's shoes!

"Hey, lady?"

"What?" she yelped.

The old man stepped back, "Geez, lady, didn't mean to scare you! I just thought you needed some help."

"No thanks! I'm fine." She jerked the car door open.

"I just wanted to—"

Without waiting for him to finish, she slammed the door shut and drove off, swerving to avoid an SUV that pulled in front of her.

#

A daunting task lay in front of Allison as she sat on the chaise in her bedroom and made a list of what to put into storage and what to leave for Kent. The painting he bought for her when they were in Paris hung on the wall next to her.

"I am not leaving that for him! It was a gift to me!" How could her life have changed so miserably?

Ring. Ring. No caller I.D. displayed.

"Hello?"

"Allison Rogers?"

"This is she."

Click.

"Oh hell!" She returned to the chaise and continued her work on the list. Although it was painful dissecting their memories, she continued until every item in the library and bedrooms, was on the list.

Without dinner and drained of all emotion, she showered and climbed into bed. Allison fell into an exhausted sleep.

Another call woke her.

"Hello?"

"Allison Rogers?"

"Yes?"

Click.

She slammed the receiver back into the cradle.

The next time the phone rang she answered, "What do you want?"

"That's a nice way to greet your sister!"

"Emma!"

"What was that about? You okay?"

"Some moron's been making crank calls. I thought he was calling back. Emma, my nerves are shot!"

"I could tell. I was in a dead sleep and woke with a start. I felt you needed me."

"I'm glad you called, Emma. By the way, what time is it?"

"It's four a.m. here in Florida." Emma got to the point of her call. "Allison, is there any way you can move back to Florida sooner?"

"I would love to, but I have more things to pack and loose ends to tie up."

"What about Kent? Where is he?"

"He's staying in a hotel. It's the way I want it. He'll come back to the house after I leave." A call beeped in. No caller I.D.

"Do you have to get that?"

"No. I'm sure it is the same jerk who called before.""Allison, do you think it's Kent?"

"I don't think so. No, I'm sure it's not. I don't know."

"So, why stay there any longer when you can be home with me?"

After the call, Allison sighed with relief. Her sister was right. She could leave before the divorce was finalized. If her attorney needed her, she would fly back. However, it would take a couple more weeks to sort through everything.

#

A harried Allison made her way through the grocery store and bought only the necessities. This was her last week in California. She left the cart to get a quart of milk. When she returned, "Where did that come from?" If it wasn't for her sweater draped over the handle, she would have thought it was someone else's cart.

"Excuse me," Allison said to the woman next to her who struggled with a small fussy child. "Did you put this bag of dog food in my cart by mistake?"

"No, I didn't!" She wiped the baby's runny nose. "I don't even have a dog!"

"I don't either." Allison removed the bag of Ol'Roy only to discover several boxes of rat poison underneath.

"Allison. Allison Rogers!"

She turned. That voice! What the hell's going on? Rattled, she left her cart where it was and rushed from the store.

CHAPTER SIX

Pinellas County, Florida

The flight from California arrived twenty minutes late to the Tampa Airport. Allison rode the shuttle to the main terminal, her excitement grew in anticipation of seeing her sister. Emma was her best friend, confidante, and sometimes, stand-in mother. Making her way to the baggage belt, she recalled how often Emma came to her rescue. *If only I had taken her advice about Kent.*

"Alli!" Emma waved to her sister.

"Oh my God. Emma, you look fabulous. What are you now, a size four?"

"No, actually a size six. But thank you for noticing." They chuckled and hugged as their eyes welled up with joyful tears.

"Hey, the belt's started. I see my bags right there in front."

"We'd better hurry, Allison. The driver is waiting."

The humidity hit Allison as they stepped outside. "I don't know if I'll ever get used to this Florida weather after living in California for six years."

Parked curbside was a limousine Emma had hired to take them home. After the driver collected Allison's luggage, they were on their way.

"Emma thanks for convincing me to come home now. I wanted

to wait until after the divorce, but I couldn't stand the stress and the god awful quiet in that big house." Allison shook her head. "I can't believe I caught Kent with a guy."

"I can't believe it, either. Kent Rogers, super-macho-mister-baseball-hero-to-the-world! And, with a rookie no less!"

"I was in shock, but you should have seen the expression on HIS face! He was absolutely white and that was before I saw who was with him."

"Allison, this isn't the right time to say I told you so, but, I will anyway." Emma squeezed her hand and they continued their ride in silence.

The Courtney Campbell Causeway was a long stretch of road connecting Hillsborough to Pinellas County. Allison caught a glimpse of a pod of dolphin breaking the surface of the blue water as they crossed over Tampa Bay. She always felt like she was home when she saw the bay. Now it was home. California and all that it reminded her of were far behind.

"I can't believe how Clearwater has built up," Allison said as they drove under the overpass at the Bayside Bridge. "What a beautiful gothic style office building. Wonder what the rent is in a place like that?"

"Allison, you're not thinking of setting up shop already?"

"No! Not at all. I told you I have given up my practice. The incident in my office cured me. But, I've always wanted to write a book about the benefit of true psychics. When Aunt Freda was bilked by a phony clairvoyant, I decided to change the format of the book to uncover psychic frauds and show how they con their unsuspecting victims!"

"Sounds pretty involved. Where do you begin?"

"I have some good ideas, but I have to work out the kinks. Let's get home and unwind first. I'll fill you in later."

Emma pointed to the billboard advertising the Rays baseball team. "You know, Allison, we have a great team here with the Rays and I've kept the season seats that Harry and I had. We might even win the pennant again this year!"

"Baseball, season tickets, Florida, and my sister, all in one day—not necessarily in that order, mind you!" Allison aimed the a/c vent toward her. "That sounds like a plan!"

"And, we have parking passes in the close lot."

"Emma, maybe we should park farther away to burn some of the calories we're going to consume at the game," Allison teased.

"I'd agree with you on that, but when the season started, some guy was murdered near the baseball dome in a remote lot. And I mean really murdered. Mutilated, burned, the whole nine yards!"

"Holy crap, Emma! You win. We'll park close."

As they approached the entrance to the house, Allison recalled the sorrow she felt the last time she entered these doors. It was for Harry's funeral last year. She admired her sister's stoic acceptance of his death, however, she knew Emma still grieved. Allison hoped moving in with Emma would be good for both of them.

"Welcome home, little sister!"

Allison stopped in the doorway of the bedroom. "Emma! I cannot believe you did all of this in such a short time." Photos of their best childhood memories lined the dresser. "Where did you find these pictures?" She started to laugh. "And look at the hair styles! What were we thinking?" Allison gently touched the faces in one of the photos. "Mom and Dad's wedding picture," she whispered. "She was so beautiful. He was so athletic. I resemble Dad a lot, don't I?"

She picked up the picture. "God, it was awful the way he died. I don't remember much about that night except for the dream."

"I remember it all," Emma said. "Mom and I were in her room. We both felt that something bad had happened to Daddy." Emma's voice cracked. "Then, you burst into the room, screaming! You said you had a bad dream that Daddy was covered in blood! You were so shaken it took a long time for Mom to calm you down."

"And, we slept in Mom's bed that night." Allison blinked back tears. "Do you think we could have stopped it, Emma?"

"Mom tried for hours but couldn't reach him."

Allison reflected, "I will never forget the expression on Mom's face when Uncle Ivan came to the house and said there had been a car accident and Dad was dead." Allison placed the photo back on the dresser. "When Mom saw us on the stairs, she knew that we heard that Daddy bled to death. She would have wanted to shield us from that horrible reality, but . . ."

"We're getting maudlin here." Emma walked to the window. "Today's about fresh starts," and opened the drapes. "Before I go, you need help to unpack?"

"Not yet. But just wait until the moving van arrives next week."

"I'm sure I have a previous engagement. If not, I'll be sure to make one!" Emma added, "Why don't you get settled in and I'll fix dinner." She gave Allison a big hug.

The warmth of her sister's touch released the months of pent up tension Allison held inside. She began to weep. All at once, the rigid tightness which had surrounded her was set free. She burst out in heart wrenching sobs. When she caught her breath, she squeezed Emma's hand and whispered, "Thanks."

"We shouldn't have brought up Dad."

"It's not that. I thought I was losing my mind these last months." Allison summarized the bizarre events that occurred when her office had been broken into, the voice at the marina, and finding dog food and rat poison in her shopping cart. "I never had a dog after Rusty died and I wouldn't ever use rat poison! None of it makes any sense."

"Do you think this has something to do with your divorce?"

"I doubt it. So far, Kent's been quite civil."

"Haven't you picked up anything intuitively?"

"No, unfortunately I've been more upset than psychic." This wasn't the time for Allison to reveal to her sister the sense of dread that shadowed her. She'd wait until she was certain that what she was feeling wasn't just a bad case of nerves.

CHAPTER SEVEN

It was not his lifelong ambition to place porcelain onto metal to make dental crowns. It did, however, make him feel less of a failure after he flunked out of dental school.

He had finished the last case of the day when his boss, Allen Dakota, entered his work space. *What's he want now? Stay late again? Come in early? How about a 'thank you' sometime.*

"Those crowns ready yet?"

"All done." He handed the box to his boss who looked inside.

"This bridge is perfect. Your work is beautiful." His supervisor patted him on the shoulder. "You're the best ceramist I've got!"

Fuck me! This is a first—a compliment! He ought to say thanks to his boss but the words wouldn't come—he nodded to Mr. Dakota. At last someone admitted to his skill. He couldn't wait to tell her. The good Karma was flowing.

He hung his lab coat on the door, eager to get home to celebrate his new-found respect. He'd pick up the fun car, put the top down, drive to Spoto's for a—"

Laughter erupted from the magpies in the hall. "He fell for that?"

Curious, he poked his head around the corner. What was so funny?

". . . Yeah, Dakota told him how great his work is just so he can ask him to work the holiday by himself."

"The boss sure can blow smoke up an ass, huh?"

"The freak will do it!"

Sarah the new girl said, "Yeah, but he really does nice work," she snorted, "for a guy with fingers like breakfast sausages!"

"Sarah, do you think it's true what they say about the size of a man's fingers and his dick?"

"I'm not sure, but in his case, I'd never want to see for myself!"

He caught his breath. The ridicule punched him in the chest. He balled his fists and stumbled back into his office.

"You cackling whores. You have no idea what these hands are capable of, or my dick for that matter. You fucking bitches have no idea who I am!"

CHAPTER EIGHT

The Rays and the Red Sox are always a sell-out. It was almost six-thirty. It wouldn't be long before people would have to park in the remote lot near Tropicana Field. Allison pulled into the private section across the street from Gate 4. This was her first game of the season. She started to rush along with the large group of people now crossing at the light.

"Umph!" Allison blurted out as a robust woman bumped her from behind and rushed past her to the gate without so much as an apology.

"Oh, gosh, I'm sorry!" an embarrassed Allison exclaimed after she stepped on the foot of the man next to her. "That lady just plowed into me. Is your foot okay?"

"Sure. Sure. Just don't let it happen again," the man said with a pained smile.

Allison was swept up in the mob going through security, excited to get to the game. She entered the baseball dome and took a deep breath. She loved the smell of baseball food and could practically taste the foot-long hot dog already. How much of her love of baseball was the game, or was it the food?

Emma hadn't exaggerated. She said these were great seats and sometimes foul balls flew over the net.

Allison answered the vibrating cell, "Emma, where are you?"

"I'm stuck here in Tampa and I'm not going to make the game."

More than a little disappointed, Allison finished the conversation and placed her purse and jacket on her sister's empty seat. A tall man with a tray of food and drink squeezed by and took his seat on the other side of her.

"Hey, how's your foot?"

"It's fine; nothing a corrective shoe won't fix." He smiled.

She apologized again. "My name's Allison." She reached out to shake his hand; hers almost disappeared into his.

"Nice to meet you. I'm Steve."

Throughout the night they shared their mutual knowledge of obscure baseball trivia.

"You sure do know a lot about baseball, for a girl."

Allison yelled at the home plate umpire. "Aw, come on, blue!"

By the seventh inning, she discovered Steve was divorced and lived in St. Petersburg. She told him she'd just moved from California and was living with her sister in Clearwater. He opened his wallet to buy beer. Allison saw a badge.

"So you're a cop?"

"Yeah, I'm a detective with the Sheriff's Office," and quickly changed the subject to baseball. "I like sitting behind home plate and try to get tickets in this section when I get to a game. How about you?"

"My sister Emma and her husband—"

"I got it!" he yelled, and shot up to catch a foul ball hit by Evan Longoria. "Here you go," he said, then handed it to her.

"For me? Wow, thanks. My first major league baseball!"

"If you want, after the game I'll take you to get that autographed."

They chatted outside of Gate 2 while they waited forty-five minutes for the players to come out to sign autographs.

"Sorry," Steve said, as he handed her the ball. "I didn't know it would take so long getting that signed."

"I didn't mind." She cradled the ball in her hands. "How cool is this! An Evan Longoria autograph!"

They continued their conversation in front of Tropicana Field, stalling their departures. After an awkward minute he asked how he could get in touch with her. Allison felt a warm flush as she wrote her number on the ticket stub.

"It's kinda late." Steve took his keys from his pants pocket. "How 'bout I walk you to your car?"

"Sure," she said with a flirtatious smile. "That would be nice. We don't have a long walk though, I am just across the street."

There weren't many vehicles around this long after the game.

"Where are you parked?" she asked.

"Way over there," he nodded toward the overpass. "I avoid game day traffic whenever I can."

The interstate overpass loomed in the background. It reminded her of the story her sister told her. She asked him if he was familiar with the gruesome murder that happened near here.

"Yeah, I know about it." He told her it was a random incident but was curious as to why she wanted to know.

She blurted out before she thought, "Steve, I'm psychic and curious to see if I could pick up anything from the crime scene. And, since we're here, maybe we could walk over there. I thought——"

"What? You're what? No you're not." He stopped short of laughing. "Not something I want to do. Anyway, this is St. Pete P.D. territory so I can't offer you any help."

"Don't worry," she forced a smile, "I didn't ask for your help," then took off in the direction she was drawn. She felt him watching her and turned. "Do you want to join me?"

"Do I have a choice?" He hurried to catch up. "It's almost midnight. You shouldn't be out here by yourself."

The lot was empty. Under the overpass it was dark and quiet with the exception of cars driving above.

He followed her as she approached an area near a pillar to the overpass. "This isn't the right place," Allison mumbled. Steve seemed annoyed and didn't respond.

"Never mind, I have it now. It's over there." She walked toward a small junk pile. "I smell chemicals." She started to cough. "No. Gasoline! I feel like I'm choking. And now flames!" She caught her breath at the unexpected horror of her psychic impressions. "The victim was beaten until his bones were broken. My God! He was burned alive!" She tried to clear the vision from her mind. "The cruelty was calculated and somehow . . . justified."

"What the hell are you talking about?"

Steve was agitated but she was positive he knew what she meant.

"The murder that took place here—what else would I be talking about?" She was accustomed with law enforcement attitude when it came to psychics and even understood their criticisms. She had hoped he would be different.

With an overt gesture, he looked at his watch. "It's late. We'd better go."

She would have to let this evening with Steve end on a low note. *Why did I have to open my mouth?*

They said polite goodbyes at her car and she watched as he turned to walk away.

He stopped, "I'm sure you believe you're picking these facts from out of the cosmos, but all of what you said was in the newspaper and on television for weeks."

"Steve! They found a pouch with the stones in it. The pouch means something. It's connected to the murderer."

Uh . . . okay . . . right. I'll be sure to let somebody know."

Allison heard him mutter "wing nut" as he left.

CHAPTER NINE

By the time the sun came up the next morning, Allison was in her car and on her way to the scene of the murder near Tropicana Field. *Allison, what the hell are you doing? You promised yourself!* But, there was an inexplicable pull drawing her there.

The place appeared so different in the daylight. In the months after the murder, there was no visible trace left of the tragic event, yet, she was drawn to the energy left behind.

She stood alone at the site. Intuitive pictures appeared within her mind's eye like images in a kaleidoscope; they were too rapid for her to sort. She concentrated to slow the stream of what she saw. Baseball cap. Black car. Star of David.

She moved to several spots, rubbing her hand through the weeds and in the dirt to psychometrize the ground. The only emotion she picked up was that of the victim—sheer terror. No emotion from the killer. No robbery. No drugs. She was positive the victim didn't know the lunatic who killed him.

Allison walked the area and mulled over what she had garnered from the energies left behind by the horrific incident. Dismayed, she paced the field. She tried to convince herself she should give the information she gleaned to the police. She knew what she'd be up against. Maybe they already have all of this information. Maybe they don't. Maybe I should just mind my own business."

She sat in the car. "Oh, hell! Maybe they'll welcome my help! Just do it!" She drove to the St. Petersburg Police Department.

"I need to speak with someone about the murder that took place near Tropicana Field a few months ago."

The officer at the desk stopped writing. "Yes ma'am. Are you a witness?"

"Well, not exactly. But I think I can help."

"Have a seat. Someone will be right with you." He motioned her to a bench in the reception area.

The officer placed a call then jotted something down. People came and went, and a couple of uniformed officers passed by, giving her a cursory glance. It seemed like hours, but only ten minutes had passed. She waited another five minutes, then reached into her purse for her car keys and stood to leave. *This was a stupid idea!*

"Ma'am, can you come here, please?"

The cop at the front desk wrote her name on a Visitor's Pass and then directed her down the hall to the open door to the Homicide Division. The desks were placed close to each other. Conversations were heard from every direction; the atmosphere, kinetic. Allison was motioned to a desk at the far end of the room by a guy in plain clothes.

"I'm Detective Gannon. What can I do for you?"

"This is going to sound strange at first, but please hear what I have to say."

His face was expressionless as he sized her up. "Go ahead."

"I'm a professional psychic and—"

"Ma'am," he said, "we appreciate you comin' down here, but we don't use psychics. So, unless you're a witness that saw something for real—"

"Detective, you don't understand. I'm not seeking a reward or publicity. I have information on a murder."

"Were you there? Did you see it take place? Did somebody tell you somethin'?"

32

"Of course, not! I saw it psychically."

"Yes, ma'am." He made a call. "Hey, Josh. I've got another psychic here with a vision. I need you to take a statement."

Laughter came through the phone loud enough to annoy her. "Detective, this may be funny to you, but I don't find it amusing."

"Yes, ma'am. Excuse me. Somebody will be here in a minute to take your statement." He cleared his throat and left.

Heads turned in her direction. Some laughed.

A young officer approached. "I'm here to take your statement."

She got up from her chair, "Don't bother!" and stormed past the rows of desks.

Assholes!

CHAPTER TEN

The remainder of her boxes arrived from California. After the truck had been unloaded, Allison watched it pull away, and was beset by conflicted emotions—sadness, relief, and optimism.

"Allison!" Emma called to her sister, "I have a great idea." She approached Allison who stood in the driveway, staring after the truck. Emma placed her hand on Allison's shoulder. "Let's do brunch at the Don Cesar tomorrow. And maybe we can catch a movie."

It was a beautiful Sunday morning and all of the guests were dressed up for brunch at the famous hotel. The sisters enjoyed a gourmet meal poolside then took a drive around town. Allison pointed to the Beach Theater. "Do they still run those wonderful classic movies?"

"Are you kidding? I just saw La Vie En Rose there and cried like a baby." Emma sang several bars of the title song in French.

"Emma, please! Don't' ruin it for me!"

"Very funny!"

They parked in front of the ticket booth and saw a young man place a 'Matinee Sold Out' sign in the window.

"I suppose we'll have to catch a weepy movie here next week."

Allison reached into her purse and pulled out her notepad. "I'll just write a reminder to call for movie times."

"Oh, for God's sake, Allison, do you still make those lists?"

"Have to. It keeps me on track. Hey," she pointed to a sign hung over a doorway, "pull over!"

"What? Why?"

"Come on." She turned to her sister and smiled. "We've got to do it!"

Emma pulled the car into the nearest space then sighed. "I can't believe I'm doing this."

On the sidewalk, Allison held her sister by the arm to make sure she didn't turn back. They walked up to the storefront and entered the shop. The window was draped with dark purple curtains and inside the air heavy with incense. Large amethyst geodes were positioned in two corners of the waiting room. Signs that directed patrons to 'De-stress' before their readings were posted in several locations. A large woman wearing a caftan greeted them.

"Well, ladies. I see you're out enjoying this beautiful Sunday afternoon. How nice of you to stop by. My name's Raven and I'm a clairvoyant."

"We're Allison and Emma." They followed her down the hallway. Emma squinted her eyes at Allison who bit her lip so she wouldn't giggle.

Raven started the psychic consultation by asking them to hold their questions until she finished. She told Allison to brace herself because her pet had a terminal disease and would die soon; in time their families would accept their unique relationship; and, this vacation the two of them are on would do their romance a lot of good! After fifteen minutes of her insights, the reading concluded with no questions asked by the 'couple.' They thanked her and left barely able to control themselves at the comical absurdity.

"That was the best entertainment I've had in a long time for twenty bucks!"

"You see! All jokes aside, people like Raven are the reason psychics are ridiculed. This is what I'm going to reveal in my book."

"Allison, I have an idea. Before we head back, how about a drive along beach?"

"If you don't mind, Emma, I'm ready to go home." Allison was deep in thought as she stared out of the window.

"Allison, you haven't said a word for the last twenty minutes. What's going on in that head of yours?"

"It's Kent."

"You're not doubting your decision to divorce?"

"No way! I'm positive it's the right thing. I've closed that chapter of my life, but thoughts of him keep popping into my head. It's a peculiar situation."

"Well, I despise him for what he did to you."

"It may sound odd Emma, but I don't hate him. To tell you the truth, I wish him well, but far, far, away!"

CHAPTER ELEVEN

Los Angeles County, California

"That damn curandera!" Carlos Dominguez sat at his kitchen table filing the barrel of the Remington 870 shotgun. He'd cut it down to sixteen inches.

The house was dead quiet. He pushed the button on the tape recorder.

". . . I only tell you what I see." He took the cassette from the machine and smashed it under the heel of his boot.

"Why'd she tell on me?"

He walked through the empty house, room by room.

"She took everything!" He punched the wall with his fist. "I only loved you, Christina." He began to sob. "Oh, Dios."

He went to the bedroom where he fell onto the bed, depressed and drunk. It was afternoon when he woke, dressed in the clothes he wore the day before. At the kitchen table he sat down, picked up a pen and wrote on the lined tablet.

For my wife and children, he began. He wrote three pages of rambling excuses, expressions of love, and apologized for what he was about to do. He ended the note; the curandera did this to me!

He placed the note on the table, loaded the shotgun and drove to Brentwood. He wove around lawn service trucks then pulled onto the circular driveway. He side-swiped the Porsche. Carlos took the shotgun and walked to the front door. He rang the bell several times. The door opened. .00 buck shot tore into Kent Rogers' chest.

"You take my wife, I take your husband. See how that feels, curandera!"

He pumped the shotgun; *click, click*. The spent shell casings flew from the gun and flipped into the flower bed.

He drove home and carried the gun to the bedroom, put the barrel into his mouth, and pulled the trigger.

#

Pinellas County, Florida

Allison grew apprehensive at the intensity of concern she felt about Kent. She called him several times before her tennis lesson. It was early in California. He should be home.

She left a voicemail. "Kent? It's Allison. I need to talk to you."

Kent hadn't returned her calls. It was difficult to pay attention to her game. She turned to her tennis instructor, "John, I've got to take a break. Give me ten minutes, okay?" She left the court and called Kent, again.

When she didn't get a response, she ended her lesson early.

Allison tried to reach him throughout the day, but could only leave messages on the answering machine. The fact he was her soon-to-be ex, didn't matter. She'd do this for anyone.

"Kent, I'm worried. Please pick up."

It was almost five o'clock when Allison came into the house with a bag of groceries in her arms.

"Sorry I'm late, Emma, but I stopped to pick up a couple of filets for dinner tonight." She unloaded the bag then turned when Emma entered the kitchen. Allison was alarmed by the expression on her sister's face. "What's wrong?"

"A Detective Beau Massaro called from California. He said he needs to talk to you as soon as possible."

"Why?"

"It can't be good. Kent's housekeeper gave him this number."

Allison got the detective on the line.

"Mrs. Rogers, is there someone with you?"

"Yes. What's this about?"

"Your husband, Kent . . . he's been shot."

"Omigod! Is he all right?"

"No Ma'am, he's not. I'm sorry to tell you this, but he was already deceased when the paramedics arrived."

"What happened?"

"We don't know much yet, but we're working on it. The homicide took place earlier today."

"This morning?" The shock was too much for her. She dropped the phone. Emma picked up the receiver and spoke to Detective Massaro, then hung up.

"He's dead, Emma! Kent's dead!" She fell into Emma's arms. "I couldn't reach him, I couldn't reach him."

CHAPTER TWELVE

Allison understood that the interview with the local detective to discuss Kent's murder was routine in these matters. On the way to the Sheriff's department, she shared with Emma—this meeting would be anything but Standard Operating Procedure.

The drive to the Pinellas County Sheriff's Office seemed to take forever. A car passed. How can those people talk? And those women: shopping as if nothing's changed. It was surreal. Kent was dead.

Upon their arrival, Allison and Emma were given visitor's passes. They were escorted to a small office where Detective Williams waited.

"Mrs. Rogers, thank you for coming down. This must be a difficult time for you." He motioned Emma to the door. "Can you excuse us, please? I need to speak with Mrs. Rogers alone."

"I'll wait right here in the hall." Emma gave her a squeeze on the shoulder as she left the room.

Detective Williams closed the door and sat behind his desk. "Mrs. Rogers, are you comfortable? Would you like a glass of water?"

"I'm okay, thank you."

"We just want you to know everything's being done to find the person who did this to your husband." She nodded. "I understand

Detective Massaro from the L.A.P.D. has set up a meeting with you."

"Yes, that's right."

"Mrs. Rogers, he's asked me to get some very basic history from you before he arrives. Do you feel up to it? It won't take very long."

"Yes, detective, whatever I can do to help."

He relaxed his pose. "Do you know of any reason someone would want to harm your husband?"

"No. But, it's all I've been thinking about."

He rifled through some papers, "When was the last time you spoke with him?"

"I haven't spoken to him since I left California."

He stood, walked to the water cooler, and filled a paper cup. "You sure you don't want a glass of water?" She shook her head. "You were going through a divorce. Is that correct?"

"Yes." She rubbed her forehead.

He returned to his seat. "Mrs. Rogers, we have knowledge of several messages you left for your husband around the time he was murdered."

Allison bristled at the condescension in his tone.

"Can you tell me why you wanted to reach him?"

She tried to describe her abilities and her psychic premonition.

"That's very interesting." He cleared his throat. "Mrs. Rogers, I see you're tired. We can stop here, for now." He rose, walked to her chair, and extended his hand. "I'm sorry for your loss. You take care and thanks again for coming in."

"Emma, I can feel that he doesn't believe me. Worse, he thinks I had something to do with what happened!"

#

The encounter at the Sheriff's Office had left her spirit depleted. By the time she reached home, her uneasiness had turned to fear. She went straight to her room, fell across the bed, and looked at the photograph on the night stand. *Mom and me.* Mom always knew the right words to comfort her. "Why would this happen, Mom? Why would the Universe give me this ability and not allow me to save Kent? It's not fair!"

She pleaded, "God! How could you let this happen? Are you punishing me?" She questioned why, for so many years, she could see events for strangers, but couldn't see this coming for herself. "Why, God? Why don't I have control over what I see?"

She wiped her eyes; her voice childlike in defeat. "It's too late for answers, Kent's dead." The specter of doom clutched her as she began to fathom the enormity of her circumstances and the possible consequences. "How can I convince them I'm not involved?"

#

Detective Massaro, a twenty-year veteran of the Los Angeles Police Department, was seated at his desk when the call came in from Pinellas County, Florida. He took careful notes while Detective Williams filled him in on the Allison Rogers' meeting.

"In my opinion," Detective Williams rattled off, "she's a looney tune; she talked about visions of murders and even claims to hear voices and smell odors. I believe she knows something but I couldn't get much out of her about her husband. Says she called him because she had a bad feeling on the day he got hit. Claims she sensed it in her mind. Sounds more like she hired a hit man and chickened out!"

"What about her alibi?" Massaro asked.

"Checks out. She was playing tennis; lots of witnesses. That's the best I can do. One cop to another, I think she's involved."

#

The local Crime Section of the <u>Los Angeles Times</u> reported the story about the body of a man found in Studio City, an apparent suicide. Police questioned his family members and were told he was despondent over his recent divorce and financial difficulties.

The police report mentioned a suicide note found, that confirmed the accounts. The investigation into the death of Carlos Dominguez was closed.

CHAPTER THIRTEEN

Pinellas County, Florida

He held the piece of mail and with a pained look of disgust, lowered his hands. Dad always teased him about his short fingers.

"Fuck you, Dad! They're your genes!" he sputtered. He tore open the envelope which bore no return address and found a folded note together with a newspaper clipping which read:

> The dismembered body of Joe K. McCoy was discovered by the Lutz police late Thursday night after they received a call from a neighbor who reported a foul smell coming from McCoy's apartment.
>
> Police spokesperson, Josie Wojcik, told reporters "McCoy was last seen Friday leaving the Four Queens Bar around midnight with another man. No further details are available. This is an on-going homicide investigation."

Handwritten on the note:

Well Done!

He smiled with satisfaction, "She's proud of me."

#

The number on the caller I.D. was too familiar. She didn't want to take the call but there was little choice. She picked it up on the fourth ring.

Without social amenities, he started right in. "I got your note. I think I did everything the way you wanted. But, I don't feel peace like you said I would . . . like I did the first time. What went wrong?"

"You're not following the rules!" she barked. "This discussion cannot take place!"

"Okay, okay!" he said. "But can you just tell me why I felt so good before?"

"Suffice it to say that you were given a small sample of the way you will feel when you have fulfilled your destiny."

"But, when will—"

Click.

CHAPTER FOURTEEN

After Allison finished speaking with Kent's brother, Ian, she made the decision not to attend Kent's memorial service. The last thing she wanted was to be a hypocrite. After all, they were going through a divorce as she had been reminded by both Ian and the Pinellas County detective.

The box in her closet was filled with old photographs and albums that she brought from California. She rummaged through it until she found what she was searching for—the picture she kept on her office desk. The one taken in Maui. *We were so happy then. Now you're dead.*

She paced around the room and held the framed photograph of them. "Why?" she whispered. She needed to know who did this to the man she once loved. Everything she picked up psychically from the picture was ordinary. The one certainty she had was that Kent and his killer didn't know each other.

Over the next few days, Allison moped around the house, overwhelmed with the blues. She continued to search through other photographs with the desire to do for herself what she'd done for so many others. Find answers!

Emma knocked on her door. "Get cleaned up, and get dressed, little sister! We're going out!"

When Allison heard Emma's insistent tone, she acquiesced. A

short time later, they were on the road going to the Beach Theater for a matinee showing of <u>The Egg and I</u> with Fred MacMurray and Claudette Colbert.

"Can you believe that, Emma?" Allison nodded across the street. "The psychic shop we went to is closed."

"Gee, isn't that amazing. And, she was o-o-oh, so-o-o good."

"Are you talking about Raven?" the freckle-faced ticket seller interrupted. He left the booth and ran to the door to take their tickets. "She was just arrested for running a whore house over there. Man, there were all kinds of cops!"

Allison winked at her sister, "I've found my first assignment, the madam Raven."

#

The next afternoon Allison opened the door to L.A.P.D. Detective Massaro and his partner, Detective Lily Totah. She was put-off to see a Pinellas County uniformed deputy with them. A fact-finding visit with the detectives from California should not have included the county deputy.

"Good afternoon, Mrs. Rogers. I'm sure you're busy so we'll try to make this brief. We just have a couple of follow-up questions about your husband's murder."

A knot in her stomach signaled trouble. She showed them into the living room. The detectives sat across from her. The uniformed deputy chose to stand which made Allison ill at ease.

"I told the Pinellas detective all I know. I can't think of anything else I can add."

"I apologize, Mrs. Rogers. You've answered a lot of questions already for the Sheriff's Office, but most of ours are routine. Just answer them as honestly as you can."

She saw through the soft-spoken 'Colombo' demeanor of Detective Massaro and felt the hostility that emanated from his partner, Detective Totah. Allison knew these questions would be anything but routine.

"I'm sensitive to what a difficult time this is for you, Mrs. Rogers. But, bear with me, please."

An hour later, Allison, exhausted from the ordeal, said, "I do not wish to be rude, but I have answered these questions before. You have humiliated me by your repeated questions about my husband's affairs. I cannot see how a discussion about our intimate sex life helps. I am not comfortable with your innuendo."

"I understand this can feel intrusive, Mrs. Rogers, but I'm only doing my job."

Detective Totah, who had been observing, excused herself and left the room to make a call. She returned and walked to the sofa, sat next to Allison and looked directly at her. Totah's posture was that of a cobra, coiled and ready to strike.

"Mrs. Rogers, can you tell me about the messages you left on your husband's answering machine," Totah stated.

"I have given you an explanation!"

"Are you sure you had no knowledge of the murder before it took place?"

"Of course not!"

"Didn't mean to rile you, Mrs. Rogers." Totah leaned back into the sofa cushion. "I meant, you being a fortune teller-or do you prefer being called a psychic—I thought you could tell us something we didn't already know."

Allison fumed. "Wha—"

"Mrs. Rogers," Massaro took over, "have you had any revelations? Is there anything you'd like to share with us?"

"In spite of the fact that I am aware you do not believe that someone can have a sixth sense, I will give you my impressions. If there is anything I can tell you that will help find Kent's killer, I will tolerate your ridicule!" She refused to allow Detective Totah to intimidate her and spoke directly to Massaro.

"I studied Kent's photograph. This is what I saw—I am sure Kent and the killer were not acquainted. The man who murdered him came by himself, had black hair and an average build. I never saw his face. He didn't care that he left the shell casings behind. And, I sensed he may have been drunk."

Massaro asked without expression, "What makes you think that?"

"I smelled alcohol."

"This man you say your husband didn't know," Totah coughed, "is he known to you?"

"NO! I said I didn't see his face!"

"Mrs. Rogers," Massaro broke in again, "is that all you can tell us?"

"Well, he may be connected with a lawn service company because I heard equipment like lawnmowers or tree trimmers. And, I smelled freshly cut grass."

"Mrs. Rogers, would you agree to submit to a polygraph?" Totah smirked as she waited for Allison's response.

Allison stood and returned Totah's gawk. "You want me to do what?" She walked straight to the foyer and opened the door.

"Detectives, I appreciate your diligence in your attempt to find who murdered Kent. And, as you say you are doing your job . . . but, unless you have a reason to insinuate that I may be involved in his death, or you intend to arrest me, this discussion is over!"

Massaro closed his notebook and walked to the door, followed by Totah. Detective Massaro nodded. "Mrs. Rogers, thank you for your time."

The deputy who had been silent, at last spoke. "Have a nice day, Mrs. Rogers."

She slammed the door behind them and leaned against the wall.

Massaro stopped at the car and gave his partner a scathing what-the-fuck-did-you-do look. "Detective Totah, you just blew any chance of cooperation from Mrs. Rogers. Next time we see her, she'll be lawyered-up."

CHAPTER FIFTEEN

In the weeks that followed her interrogation with the police about Kent's murder, Allison's life settled into a routine. She moved forward with her decision to write a book. More determined than ever, she began with 'Raven, the madam.'

#

Emma asked, "Who called?"

"I got the best news! That was Marilyn Miller from Channel Six. Remember I told you that I finished the story on Raven and two fake psychics I learned about and the schemes they used? Marilyn pitched my work to the program director."

"Allison, take a breath and slow down."

"He likes the concept and wants me to develop it further to cover the Bay Area. The report will be featured on the 'Around Town' segment. If it's received well, the station would consider running reports that would cover the state. Emma, this could lead into something big! Who knows? I could be the next Barbara Walters!"

"Allison, after all you've been through, are you sure you want to take this on now?"

"I've got to keep busy."

"I doubt you're ready for the demands a television deadline will make on you if this goes." Emma cleared the table and removed her plate with her meal half eaten.

"I thought you'd be happy for me. Why are you in such a huff?"

"First of all, a psychic with two years of writing classes in college does not a 'Barbara Walters' make. Second, are you crazy going public with your work so soon? Have you checked with a lawyer? You could get into trouble. And third, how could you let Marilyn read your story before you gave it to me?"

"Emma, this is why I didn't come to you first. As far as my investigative stories are concerned, they're acceptable for Channel Six, who, by the way, have their own attorneys. Second, I didn't expect to go public this soon. It was a fortunate, premature introduction that started all of this. And third, oh just forget it. I'm sorry you feel slighted because I asked Marilyn to read it first."

Allison took the folder off the counter and handed it to Emma, then went to the refrigerator for a carton of pomegranate juice, poured it into a plastic glass from the cabinet, and walked out to the pool.

"Can I get you a sandwich?" Emma called from the doorway.

"No thanks, Mother Dear," her tone more loving than sarcastic.

Allison gazed into the clear sparkling pool and thought of the creek alongside the home where they grew up in Ohio. The memory of the old clapboard house with its white picket fence, the grape arbor, and the truck patch with rows of vegetables; seems so long ago.

She saw Emma inside the kitchen seated at the table with the folder open reading the story. Allison remembered how she'd sit next to her sister on the sofa while Emma checked her schoolwork. The memory made Allison feel warm and fuzzy.

Emma opened the sliding glass door, "This is good! I can tell you did your homework."

"I'm glad you liked it," Allison said, with enthusiasm. "There's a lot more I want to cover, or uncover." She patted the chair beside her. "Come join me, Emma. I have a proposition for you."

"What are you up to?" She took her place next to Allison.

"This will require a lot of work. I need someone to be my investigative assistant."

"Uh-oh."

The plan was, as she described it, to visit several psychics for a reading. She had made a list of questions she'd ask each one and if she was lucky, she might be able to talk to some of their clients.

"In all fairness, I have to be objective. So, I may need 'someone' I trust to also visit these psychics so I can compare their accuracy."

"Oh, and let me guess," Emma rolled her eyes, "I am the 'someone.' Let's hope this doesn't turn out like the time you convinced me to assist you in your high school talent show. As I recall, you needed three stitches from the bite when you tried to pull off the rabbit in the hat trick. And, I had to run after the rabbit when it took off into the audience."

#

It didn't take long for a plan to take hold. Within a short time, the sisters had called on several readers. It was in one of these waiting rooms that Allison met a young couple who were in search of the psychic who had disappeared with their money. They told Allison they hoped this new psychic would help them find him.

It was quite a story Allison was told from the young husband and wife with whom she'd spoken. They claimed to have been conned by someone calling himself a 'medical intuitive' who advised them there was no need for them to pay ten thousand dollars to their fertility doctor. Instead, he assured the couple he could guarantee a pregnancy for twenty-five hundred dollars. He ensured a pregnancy in six months or they'd get a full refund. All they had to do, he said, was to wear the special amulets he would provide. Thrilled at the prospect of starting a family, they agreed and paid him the money. Six months later they returned to his office, not pregnant. They'd discovered he had skipped town.

It pained Allison that she couldn't ignore the sadness and defeat in the couple's voices. Desperate people do desperate—and foolish—things. Yet, here they sat, waiting for another reader to help them find the man who took off with their money and their dream.

CHAPTER SIXTEEN

Los Angeles County, California

"Mommy?"

"What is it, Rosie?"

"Who is, Allison Rogers?" Christina Dominguez' eyes widened at her eight-year-old daughter's question.

"Shut up, Rosie!" Carlito shouted to his sister.

"Allison Rogers is a friend of mine." Her mother concealed her distress. "Why?"

"Rosie!" Carlito banged his glass on the table, splashing milk. "I said, shut up!"

"Stop it, both of you!"

"It's mine, so shut up, Rosie, or I'll tell Mom you lost your good sweater!"

"You just did, you jerk!"

Christina took control of the situation and asked, "Why do you want to know about Allison Rogers?"

"Well, if she's your friend, how come we don't know her?"

"Because I go to see her when I need help."

"Is she a doctor?"

"No, Rosie. She's a *curandera*. That's a kind of medicine woman who has special powers and can see the past and the future. How do you know her name?"

"Daddy says her name all the time."

Christina dropped a bowl of mashed potatoes she had just removed from the table. "When did Daddy talk about Mrs. Rogers?"

"I hate you, Rosie!" Carlito ran to his room, slammed the door and locked it.

"Rosie, go wait in your room." Christina's hands trembled as she squatted to clean the mess from the floor. She dabbed at the nervous perspiration on her face before she went to her son's room.

"Carlito? I want to talk to you." She knocked again. "Carlito! Open this door!"

"No! You'll take it away!"

"Take what away?"

"I don't want to forget what Daddy sounds like!" His sobs resonated through the door. "You gave me his recorder so it's mine!"

"Carlito, let me in."

He opened the door, the tape player clutched in his other hand. Tears streamed from his swollen eyes.

"Where did you find that tape?"

"In Daddy's desk."

Christina sat on her bed and pressed 'PLAY.' "Allison. Allison Rogers." She gasped! "Carlos!" and allowed the cassette to play to the end. On the tape was her dead husband's voice repeating, 'Allison. Allison Rogers,' sometimes with anger, others without emotion like a telemarketer. The last one was filled with such bitterness, she shuddered. 'You will pay curandera.'

"Madre de Dios, Carlos!" She cried.

As painful as it was, Christina knew what she had to do. She would contact the police in the morning when she was more composed.

Her voice quivered as she introduced herself to the officer on the phone. "I found something in my husband's belongings." Her hand tightened around the cassette. "I think it might have to do with Kent Roger's murder."

"What is it, Mrs. Dominguez?"

"It's a tape recording of my husband's voice calling Allison Rogers' name." She fought back tears. "I'm not sure what to do with it."

"Did your husband confess to the murder?"

"No! He repeats her name, over and over."

"That's it, nothing else?"

"I heard him . . . there's a . . . at the end he said . . . it's probably nothing. I'm sorry I bothered you."

"It's no bother." He rushed, "Don't hang up, Mrs. Dominguez. Why don't you bring it to the station and let the detective assigned to that case make the decision."

Christina handed the cassette to the L.A.P.D. officer she had spoken to earlier. He let her know that Detective Beau Massaro had been assigned to the Rogers' case. "He's not here right now, but I'll see that he gets this." He placed the tape inside an envelope with Christina Dominguez' contact information on it, and sealed it.

"Ma'am, before you leave, is this the only tape you have?"

"No," she stammered. "The tape belongs to my son so I made him a copy. The one you have is the original."

#

Detective Massaro arrived to the office an hour earlier than usual to catch up on his backlog of cases after taking off the weekend. There he found a stack of messages and folders piled on his desk. He grabbed a cup of coffee and sat to face his day's work. He picked up an envelope from the top of the pile with the name and address of a Mrs. Christina Dominguez written on the outside. She identified the voice on the tape as her deceased husband, Carlos Dominguez.

At the bottom-RE: Kent Rogers' Homicide.

He removed the tape and opened his desk drawer. "Aw shit!" he bellowed. "Who took my goddamn tape player again?"

A young officer stopped at his desk. "Here it is. I was just about to return it."

Massaro reached for the recorder without a thank you and popped in the cassette. He played the tape through twice, then turned to his computer and typed in 'Carlos Dominguez.' The county computer system found charges listed against a Carlos Dominguez in Studio City; a couple of charges for domestic violence, and one for aggravated assault; both within the last year.

After a quick call to the Studio City P.D., Massaro discovered Dominguez killed himself with a shotgun on the day Kent Rogers was murdered with the same kind of weapon. "Interesting coincidence."

"Whatcha got there, Massaro?" Lily Totah leaned over his desk and glanced at the computer screen.

"You know, Totah, I'm beginning to believe that Mrs. Rogers is on the up-and-up."

"You mean you buy this psychic shit?"

Massaro frowned. "No. I mean I don't believe she's involved."

"Aw, come on! You've gotta know she's guilty."

"With what I see here," he pointed to Carlos Dominguez' criminal history on the computer screen, "and this," he turned on the cassette player, "I'm not so sure."

"Puleese," she begged. "She said it, herself! She catches her husband fudge-packing his boyfriend—"

"Nice mouth, Totah."

"Whatever. So, she leaves town for a good alibi, she gets a multi-million dollar house, all his life insurance, his baseball pension. She divorces him, she gets squat. The way I see it, she has more than twenty million reasons to kill him. My gut says she did it!"

"You gonna start wearing a turban and carrying a crystal ball now?"

"Fuckin'A, Massaro! I know what I'm talkin' about!"

"Totah, before you burn her at the stake, let's re-evaluate what we have. And, have them check the firing pin impact point on the Dominguez shotgun and compare it to the shell casings we found at the Rogers' shooting. Tell them I want the report yesterday. And one more thing, locate the Dominguez vehicle and have it checked for paint transfer from the Porsche. Maybe we'll get lucky."

"You know," Totah stopped at the door, "if all this shit matches, it only means she hired this Dominguez guy as the shooter."

"Then get me some evidence connecting them! Check his bank accounts, phone records, get me something!" He directed his attention back to his computer and called over his shoulder, "Hey Swami, close the door on your way out!"

CHAPTER SEVENTEEN

Pinellas County, Florida

In the months since Kent's death, Allison had investigated several more psychics. One was genuine; one was a well-meaning kook; the rest were charlatans. The first report was featured on 'Around Town' and was well received. Allison was inundated with mail and messages from victims.

More motivated than ever to expose the con artists posing as psychics, she reviewed her notes for her new segment on News Channel Six and prepared for her visit to the Psychic Fair tomorrow.

By the end of the day, between researching leads and follow-up calls, she felt as if her brain was fried. Allison concluded that if she was going to keep up with these demands she would have to become more disciplined and organized. She'd start tomorrow. What she needed now was a diversion and going to the ballgame tonight is just what the doctor ordered.

She and Emma rode to Tropicana Field with the convertible top down. Emma opened the glove box to retrieve a ball cap to cover her windblown hair.

"Allison, what's this baseball doing here?"

"Oh my, gosh, I forgot all about it. There was a guy. I stepped on his foot. He caught a ball for me and—"

"You met a man and didn't tell me?"

"To tell the truth, it was awkward. You know how you are always telling me I need to be more subtle when it comes to my psychic work?"

"Yes, I do. And you never take my advice." Emma tucked a wisp hair under the cap.

"Well, I did it again. The guy's name is Steve. He's really cute, and a cop."

"Let me guess. You confessed that you were a psychic; he didn't believe you; you were insulted, end of evening."

"Good guess. And yes, I also tried to show off." Allison teased . . . "I can hear what you're thinking."

"What?" Emma chuckled. "I didn't think anything."

"That would be a first!" Allison chortled. *Thank you, Mom. The best thing you ever did was give me my sister.*

As they entered the Dome, Allison whispered to her sister. "Remember that guy, Steve, I told you about on the way here? He just saw me." She considered speaking to him, but when he turned away . . .

"Emma, go on ahead. I'll get the boiled peanuts and be back before the National Anthem."

"Get the Cajun ones!"

Allison returned sooner than expected, empty-handed.

"Where are the peanuts? You get lost?"

"I'm so mad I could spit nickels!" She plopped down in her seat. "I can't believe what just happened."

"What's the problem?"

"I saw Steve. He was in line ahead of me deep in conversation with some guy. I didn't want to talk to him so I turned away. That's when I overheard him tell his buddy about me. Of course he exaggerated and made me sound like a real nutcase. What a liar! The longer I stood there the madder I got."

"Allison, it can't be that bad."

"I didn't get all of what they said, but I did hear Steve refer to me as a fruit loop! His face turned as red as Curt Schillings' bloody sock at the World Series when he saw me. I just walked away."

Allison turned to buy Cracker Jacks from the vendor and saw Steve take his seat. "Emma, don't turn around. He's two rows behind us!" She faced forward. "I can feel him watching. I hope he spills his beer all over his lap."

Midway through the game a loud "damn" came from behind the sisters.

"O'Keefe! You knocked over my beer!"

CHAPTER EIGHTEEN

Allison returned from her day at the Psychic Fair. The events fresh in her mind, she wrote her first draft of her story.

Psychic Fair: Booths and tables, outside along waterfront.

- Man with camera—aura photographs. No expert! Claimed he could give you aura if you didn't have one!

- Love potions and oils—ward off evil spirits.

- Numerology charts in five minutes. Find your soul mate.

- Man in gray jumpsuit—alien pins for identification when Mother Ship arrives.

- Astrologer—Professional, accurate, informative. Large sum of money coming? Physical danger to me—be alert to my surroundings for next two months.

Emma set aside her needlepoint canvas when her sister entered the sunroom. "Get much writing done?"

"Here," Allison handed her the pages she had completed. "Read for yourself."

She intended her book to be informative but more important to her she wanted to prevent another 'Aunt Freda' from losing not only their money, but their dignity.

"This is interesting, Allison. I must admit I had to snicker at the mother ship pins."

"I'm glad the astrologer saw a lot of money in my future." Allison added, "My research costs a small fortune!"

"Are you suggesting I pick up dinner tonight?"

"Yeah and maybe next week, too. There's another psychic I plan to see. It had better be worth it. This one charges two hundred an hour."

"Two hundred dollars?" Emma raised her eyebrows. "I wonder if that includes dinner. Whew! Maybe I should come out of retirement!"

"Really?"

"I'm not serious, Allison. You know that's never going to happen. So how do you approach this one? Do you suppose she's real? If so, she'll see right through you."

"I sure hope she's real for that kind of money. I want this book to prove there are gifted readers and to bring to light those who are not."

"Allison, if the rest of your work is as thorough and enlightening as this, you'll have a best seller!"

"From your mouth to God's ears! Now that you've made me a bestselling author, shouldn't we celebrate by dining out?"

"Let's try that new Thai restaurant on Enterprise Road."

#

The restaurant bustled with activity. Delicious fragrances filled the air. The sisters ordered all their favorite foods.

Before she finished her spring roll, Allison was cognizant of being observed. She perused the room which appeared to be filled to capacity. They were ordinary diners.

"Allison. What's with you?"

"I feel like I'm being watched."

Emma nodded toward the booth across the room. "Isn't that Detective Williams from the Sheriff's Office?"

"Yes, it is." She pushed her chair back from the table. "I'm going right up there and—"

"You'll do no such thing, Allison. He probably stopped in for a drink and recognized you. Leave it alone."

"I'm ready to leave anyway." On the way out, Allison made eye contact with him and nodded. "Good evening, Detective Williams."

#

One of the errands Allison had for the day was to get a long-overdue tune up for her car. She'd wait across the street in the Courthouse café until it was finished.

Her coffee had just arrived when someone said, "So we meet again. Mind if I join you?"

Caught off guard by Steve's unexpected appearance, "What are you doing here?"

"I'm a cop. We know all the good coffee places."

She thought about the last time she saw him at the concession stand. "Sure you want to have coffee with a Fruit Loop?"

"Only if you don't mind having a jerk keep you company." He slid into the opposite side of the booth. "I guess I owe you an apology."

"Yes, you do. I hope it's a quick one—I have to pick up my car soon."

"I'm sorry. I can really be a rectum sometimes." He pulled a paper napkin from the dispenser and waived it. "Truce?"

"Truce it is!"

"So . . . you doing any more television reports?"

"It's a work in progress and I'm not so sure we should talk about my profession. Have you forgotten Tropicana Field?"

"You know, Allison, I'm a skeptic. And, as a cop, something has to be tangible before I can buy into it. I'm unable, no, let me change that, I refuse to take at face value concepts as abstract or indefinable as psychic powers. I need to see it in black and white."

"Oh, you mean like gravity or radio waves? Steve, psychic ability is nothing more than an instinct we all possess, although it's more developed in some of us. Haven't you ever had a gut feeling? That's just another way of saying intuition."

His face was blank.

"Allison, in law enforcement we're trained to be observers. That doesn't make us psychic."

"Whether you believe it, doesn't change the fact that it does exist." She sipped the last of her coffee and got up. "Steve, I'd love to continue this conversation another time, but I have a mechanic waiting for me."

"No worries." Steve said with a big grin, "I have a hunch I'll be seeing you again."

CHAPTER NINETEEN

Psychic Anne Preston put the cardboard witch in the trash can and made a mental note to tell the building manager that she didn't want holiday decorations on her office door. Christmas Santas and Valentine's Day hearts were distraction enough, but she bloody well wouldn't tolerate Halloween witches.

Anne didn't like the client who was due in thirty minutes; but, money was money. She knew the woman's husband had been killed, but didn't want to deal with the drama that was about to unfold. The outer door opened.

"Bloody, FUCK! She's early."

Anne saw Grace as a disgusting excuse for a woman and moreover, a lousy mother. She felt foster care was an abomination, but Grace Chamber's daughter, Irene, had a better chance of surviving her childhood in a foster home than with this wretched woman. She sighed and opened the door to her office.

"Hello, Grace. Won't you please come in," Anne said in a forced attempt to sound pleasant.

"Why?" the distraught woman begged, and bumped into Anne as she rushed into the office. "Why didn't you tell me this was going to happen?" The woman's body shook with grief.

"Please, try to compose yourself." Anne placed her arm around Grace's back and guided her to a chair.

"Who would do this to my poor Lenny?"

Anne made no attempt to conceal the contempt she knew Grace saw.

"He wasn't perfect, Anne, but he didn't deserve to die like that! His face was burned off! We had to have a closed casket!" After a long cry, Grace quieted, although her body quivered every so often.

Over the last year, Anne counseled Grace several times and believed she had made it clear during her last reading, that their daughter had told the truth. Lenny did, in fact, rape Irene and had abused her from the age of thirteen. Yet, Grace chose to forgive Lenny rather than report him to the police as she'd promised she would.

Speechless, Anne couldn't believe her ears when Grace said how two days before his death, he cried and begged for her forgiveness for what he'd done to their daughter and swore never to touch her again. He blamed it on his alcohol and cocaine use. He pledged to God that he'd never use drugs again.

"That was a confession, Grace. You should have called the authorities."

"It wasn't all his fault, Anne! You don't understand how many times I told Irene not to prance around the house in her pj's and to keep the bedroom door locked."

This despicable woman made Anne sick. Old feelings tried to escape her suppressed memories. She wanted to scream at the insanity of what Grace said, but was without voice.

"A lot of what happened was my fault." Grace continued with her bizarre rationale. "When he started using drugs I got so depressed I let myself go. You saw me. I gained sixty pounds." Grace sobbed more. "Lenny was so sincere that he didn't want our family to break up, he went to Irene and apologized. Do you know how hard that was for him? Irene didn't care. All she did was stand there; never said a word. He loved me, Anne. He really loved me." She rubbed her eyes. "How he must have suffered."

The woman's voice resonated in Anne's head. She refused to

hear another word. *You stupid, fucking cow!*

"Grace, what is wrong with you? You must get Irene to a psychiatrist, now!"

"Why? So she can hang our dirty laundry for a stranger to see? It wouldn't be fair. Lenny isn't here to defend himself. Besides, she'll be fine. I was molested and I got over it."

Grace Chambers was in the top ten of the most debased human beings she'd had the misfortune to meet. On days like today, she questioned why a woman like this continued to live.

She's just like the one in Oregon.

The vial woman left. Anne returned to her desk and picked up the crystal paperweight. Its coolness soothed her.

"The world is a better place without you, Lenny Chambers?"

#

It had been a long, profitable, and tiresome week for Anne. It felt good to be home. She removed her clothes and shed with them, layers of emotional grime. Wrapped in a silk robe, she went to the kitchen.

From her wrap-around balcony she could enjoy both the gulf from the west side of her unit and the bay on the east. *I love the place.* She looked around her sparsely furnished apartment and regretted that she had not rented more furniture. Her life was a series of 'temporary.' That could be all for now.

"God, I love Red Zin and tonight I'll drink the whole bloody bottle."

She took a glass of wine out on the balcony. Surrounded by the reds, golds, pinks, and yellows from the setting sun reflecting off the Gulf of Mexico, she was awed by its magnificence. She put up her feet and read the Tampa Courier.

The big orange sun sizzled on the horizon and disappeared into the Gulf. Chilled in her light robe, Anne picked up the paper to move inside. A name caught her eye in the obituary column on the back page. Irene Chambers.

The article concluded with:

In lieu of flowers, donations can be made to the American Society for Suicide Prevention.

She read the name again. The paper dropped from her hands.

"Bloody fucking, Christ!" She yelled so loud her voice cracked.

Anne poured another glass of wine. Her throat stung when she swallowed. Her hand tightened around the delicate crystal glass. It shattered. Wine mixed with her blood. She felt no pain from the cut.

"Stop, stop. Please, stop." Anne couldn't block the memories. She tried to shut out the words, but failed. *Annie, Annie. Come here, baby. Uncle Johnny has something for you . . .*

CHAPTER TWENTY

He was pissed off and tired. His boss, Allen Dakota made him cram the week's workload at the lab into three days. Now it was Thanksgiving Day. He hated the holidays with all the superficial family horseshit.

"Let's eat turkey and pumpkin pie and watch fucking stupid football and act like we're all so glad to be together!"

There was no one to hear him. He was alone in his kitchen. The television was on and the Macy's Parade was underway. He examined the face of a little boy who held his father's hand. Was anything in life real? Did everyone pretend? Was happiness only for the innocent? He couldn't remember if he was ever happy.

He rubbed his scarred arms and walked into the bathroom to retrieve a razor blade. He thought the high he felt after the first sacrificial offering would last, but it didn't.

He completed his ritual and watched the blood drip into the sink along with his emotional pain. He saw himself in the mirror and remembered his promise to stop cutting. Standing in his closet in front of the full length mirror, he dressed and tugged at the cuffs of his shirt to cover his scars and spoke to his reflection.

"When will my karmic debt be satisfied?" He needed to ask her but he couldn't break the rules. He'd have to wait.

One last time, he glanced over at the book she gave him for his birthday and recited their special poem from memory. *Is she lonely too?* He wanted to see her.

He'd followed her home so many times before; he could almost do it blindfolded. If she was home, he could drop in on her. Would she invite him to share Thanksgiving dinner?

"Yeah, like that's going to happen!"

Gulf Boulevard near her apartment was an obstacle course of orange cones that directed the Turkey Trot 5K runners to the beach. He had to wait for stragglers from the race to pass before he could get close enough to her place. The last runners were out of eyesight. He parked in the shopping center across from her guard gate and walked up the beach access next to her building. He watched the balcony that he knew was hers, and saw no signs of her. His disappointment was deep; he felt a catching pain in his stomach.

Unable to bear the loneliness he returned to his car and drove without a destination in mind. He didn't want to be alone today. His life was so unfair; his innocence taken; his existence void of pleasure except for thoughts of her.

His heart raced when he spotted the dome of Tropicana Field. He hadn't been back to this place since the night he'd been reborn.

The street was deserted. He parked the car and stepped out onto the vacant lot. An emaciated dog lumbered around a pile of trash that the wind had blown into a mass of weeds next to a concrete support.

He moved at a slow pace to allow the smallest of details to register. There it was—the hallowed ground. He stood in reverent silence. Although it was mid-day, he was transported to the dark of night. He relived each step of the execution: The cracking bones. The pleading eyes. The flames.

His high had returned as she promised! He was euphoric. He was omnipotent. He wanted to sing. The effervescence of the moment convinced him he was the Chosen One!

CHAPTER TWENTY-ONE

Nine-year-old Brian Rice, dressed only in his sneakers and socks, trembled as much from fear as from the cold. The room he occupied wasn't much bigger than the van the man kept him in before he was put in the shed two days ago. The boy peeked out of the small hole in the boarded window—darkness.

Three days before, the child rode his bike near his home. The man in the white van snatched Brian and put him in a dog cage in the back of the vehicle.

Brian flinched when the shed door opened. "No, no, no!" he screamed. "Go away! MOMMY!" He scrunched himself against the wall.

His captor tossed a McDonald's bag at Brian's feet, put a six pack of beer beside him, and left. He locked the door.

Brian tore open the bag. "Hamburgers!" He chomped down the cold, stale meal, his first food in days. His little fingers tugged at the tab on top of a beer can. He was so thirsty he gulped it. Minutes later he vomited in the corner of the filthy dark place and cried himself to sleep.

It was hot when he woke and from the peephole in the board he saw the bright sun. Thirst seized him and he opened another can of warm beer. This time he made sure to drink it slow. It made him drowsy.

Brian touched his bottom. It wasn't bleeding anymore but he moaned when he moved.

"Mommy," he whimpered. "Please come get me." He fell into a deep sleep after he drank another beer.

The man returned and ordered Brian to open his mouth.

"Bite me and I'll kill you!"

When the man was done, he left a box of cheese crackers and two more cans of beer. Brian watched out of the hole as the man walked away. He drank a beer and fell asleep.

"Get off me!" he yelled, and slapped at something that bit his ear. He jumped up as a rat scampered through a hole at the bottom of the wall. Brian lay back down and kicked at the plank the rat had squeezed through.

#

The first thing Anne Preston did when she got to work was check her schedule. *A full day and a full purse.* She added Sara Rice to her schedule. No time for lunch. If it hadn't been about a missing child, she would have put her off.

Sara Rice started to talk before she sat down. "I was told you could help us. I don't know what we're gonna do. My nephew, Brian, is missing. Is he hurt? Is he alive? I need to know, did he run away? Did someone—"

"Just a minute, please," Anne said, holding up her hand to silence Sara. "This is not how I conduct my readings. As dreadful as what you are facing may be, you must allow me–"

"Miss Preston, please. You don't understand. Ain't you seen the news? There's no time to waste. Brian's gone! It's been three whole days. No word at all!" She took a deep breath. "The cops: what are they good for? They can't come up with nothin'!" Sara held out a picture. "Please, I'm begging you, tell me somethin'."

"All right Ms. Rice, but, I need time to get a clear image." Anne's solar plexus tightened. She had an intense dislike of being pressured by someone who had no understanding of how her abilities worked. She ran her fingers through her hair before she spoke. "He's been kidnapped!"

"I knew it! He wouldn't run away. He ain't that kinda kid."

Anne continued. "There's a white van. He was put in some kind of cage."

"A cage?" Sara screamed.

"Yes, a wire cage. I see a small room—"

"Where? In a house?"

Once more, Anne motioned for silence. "I see a blonde man. He's young. Maybe thirty." She lowered her head.

Sara leaned forward, "What is it? What's wrong?" and lifted out of her seat.

"Your nephew's alive and he'll be home within a week." Anne stood to signal the end of the reading.

"Oh, Sweet Jesus! He's alive!" Sara cried, "Oh, thank God! Thank God! But where is he? Is he hurt? Who did this?"

"That's all I can tell you."

"Let's go to the police."

"I don't go to the police, Ms. Rice. You may if you wish."

"But Miss Preston, you could tell them."

"I've told YOU all I can." She held the door as Sara rose to leave.

"Please, won't you—"

"I'll tell you this," Anne placed her hand on Sara's shoulder, "you'll have your little Scoots home soon."

"Omigod! That's my pet name for him. You gotta know somethin' else."

"I'm sorry, Ms. Rice. As I said before, that's all I can tell you."

Anne returned to her desk, picked up the crystal paperweight and contemplated what she had seen but hadn't shared with Sara. The family didn't need to know now what the bastard was doing to him. They'd find out soon.

#

Sara drove straight to the police station. She stepped ahead of an elderly man who waited to speak with the Desk Sergeant.

"S'cuse me, Sir. I'm Sara Rice. My nephew's the boy who got kidnapped. A psychic told me—"

"Hold on, Ma'am." The officer motioned for the old man to step forward, but the elder gentleman nodded his 'go ahead' to the distressed woman.

"Sir, this is important. A psychic had a vision about my nephew."

"I'm sorry Ma'am. We don't work with psychics. We have plenty of law enforcement officers out there trying to find your nephew."

"But, you gotta understand."

"I do. I have a son that age, myself."

"But, she knows—"

"Ma'am, I sympathize with what you're going through. We have our best people on this case. A missing child is a priority with all law enforcement."

Sara turned to leave and bumped into the old man who had moved closer to eavesdrop on her conversation.

"I'm praying for the little boy," the old man called to her as she ran out of the building.

CHAPTER TWENTY-TWO

Because of the success of Allison's reports on News Channel Six they would now be featured bi-monthly.

Tonight's show was special. Emma and Aunt Freda were in the studio. Allison's live report on Common Sense and Psychics concluded with the announcement of the arrest of Earl Cavanaugh, the man who had bilked Freda and others out of thousands of dollars.

"Sweetheart, I'm so proud of you. It was worth losing that money just to see you the star of the show!" Aunt Freda held Allison's arm as they walked down the hallway to the Green Room. "Thanks to you, Sugar, he won't steal from anyone else."

Her aunt stopped everyone backstage to brag about her niece who was going to be a star. She told them how each Christmas 'little Allison' would take a toilet paper roll and pretend it was a microphone to entertain the family. "And now, my Alli is a famous news reporter."

"Watch out, Katie Couric," Emma said, "here comes Allison Rogers."

Allison blushed at the over-exuberant praise and ushered them into the Green Room.

"Honey, this year hasn't been easy for you," Aunt Freda gave her a light pat on the cheek. "But, the stars are shining on you now."

Allison told them that her producer, Phillip, asked to speak with her. She'd catch up with them at the restaurant as soon as they were done.

"You wanted to see me, Phillip?"

"Wow, great show! And, that aunt of yours! What a hoot!"

"Yeah, that's exactly what I was thinking."

"Don't take this the wrong way, Allison, but, why didn't your aunt come to you for a reading?"

Without hesitation she said that Aunt Freda had always been an independent, strong-willed woman. She'd gone to psychics long before Allison was born. "Her neighbor convinced her that this new reader could practically walk on water . . . well, the rest is history."

"Oh, I get it." He tapped his pen on the desk. The calm and sedate Phillip, now appeared animated, almost excited. "I've talked to the powers-that-be and they'd like to use your psychic fraud exposes to develop a series on our affiliate cable station." He repeated, "Psychic Fraud Expose. Hey, that'd make a cool title. You interested?"

"Of course, I'm interested."

After a brief discussion about the format, Phillip said he'd get started on the project.

"Before you go, do you still do it?"

"Do what?"

"You know, see things. Find criminals and stuff."

"Phillip, I retired from my practice but I'm still psychic." It was unbelievable that he wasn't better informed on the subject. "Why do you ask?"

"This is a picture of the missing kid, Brian Rice," he handed her the photo. "Tell me what you get. It'd make for a good show."

"I'll see what I can do, but I don't want to make a story out of it." She turned her attention to the picture of the little boy.

"Don't be so quick to say no to a story. Your reports bump up ratings."

"The answer is no, Phillip!" Allison straightened in her chair, took a deep breath and began.

"He's been abducted by a stranger, but he'll be found alive."

"He's alive?" He stood over her. "What else?"

"There's a white camper—no, a van with tools in the back and some sort of metal crate."

"You can see all that?" his jaw dropped, "this is awesome." His voice lowered. "What else?" Phillip took notes.

"And I smell beer."

"Where is he?" Phillip pressed, "Where is he?"

"I only know it's not far from where he was taken; less than an hour. But, I can't see the exact location."

"Keep going."

She placed the picture on his desk. "I don't see anything else."

"Can't you try harder?"

"Phillip, it doesn't work that way."

"If you can see all that other stuff, how come you can't see where he is?"

She detected disappointment in his voice.

"I don't have control over what I see."

"Wish you could've seen more. It'd be great for us to find this kid. But, thanks anyway for the attempt."

She couldn't wait to get out of Phillip's office and regretted that she'd not left sooner. She felt inadequate. Mom's words, 'you're a psychic, not the Almighty,' brought her no comfort.

She reached the door to the studio exit when Phillip yelled, "Why don't you ask some of the psychics you know if they see anything about the Rice kid. It'd make a great show, even if they're wrong. We'd get good promos out of it!"

Even, if they're wrong? God, Phillip!

CHAPTER TWENTY-THREE

Brian kicked at the board until it loosened. He pushed and squeezed until he wiggled through the jagged wood. He was free of his prison. His body was scratched and bled but he'd escaped. He started to run in the dark. Trees and brush. No highway. No houses. He ran until he couldn't catch his breath. Exhausted, he fell to the ground. There were no sounds, no lights. No one followed.

At sunrise, he was jolted out of his half-conscious state. Fire ants! Biting him! He screamed and swatted them off. His naked body covered in welts. He ran again and fell on to a gravel road. He dropped to his knees and whimpered.

A forest ranger drove down the hill from the fire tower, and at the sight of the naked child, slammed on the brakes.

Brian opened his eyes in the Emergency Room. His mother was there. He saw the police, and doctors and nurses. It wasn't a dream. He was safe.

He told the deputies about how he was pulled off his bike and shoved into the back of a van, and how the man hurt him. He described the shed and said he was sorry that he drank the beer because his mother told him beer was bad. He wasn't sure what his kidnapper looked like because the man always wore a mask, but he smoked all the time. Brian told the police the van was kinda like the white one at the end of his street. The guy was sorta the same size of the new guy who lives there.

#

The initial police investigation revealed that the man who lived in the trailer park and drove the white van was Jeremy Butterworth. It also disclosed he had numerous traffic violations and a record as a juvenile for sexual battery on a child under the age of eleven. Charges were dropped. The victim wouldn't testify.

Police discovered that Butterworth had a record on Lewd and Lascivious but, that wasn't sufficient for an arrest. It was cause for suspicion. Investigators questioned his neighbors and were told Butterworth was quiet, kept to himself, and had moved into the park recently. No one ever saw him with a dog. They all complained that he dumped his ashtrays in the street.

Area sex offenders were rounded up to be questioned. Butterworth included. He did not have a verifiable alibi. During his interrogation, he gave several versions of his whereabouts during the time of the disappearance of Brian Rice. In spite of his belligerence and inconsistencies, without evidence that connected him to the abduction, he had to be released.

The police didn't reveal to Butterworth that they were aware of his suspended driver's license. Jeremy got behind the wheel of his van and pulled on to the highway. He was arrested.

He was held at the Pinellas County Jail. Deputies did an inventory search of the impounded vehicle. Cigarette butts covered the floor and a wire dog crate was found in the back of the van. That gave probable cause for a search warrant for the entire vehicle.

A warrant was obtained; traces of hair, skin, and blood were taken from the cage and sent to Florida Department of Law Enforcement for DNA analysis. With a rush on the request, it would take about a week for the results.

Butterworth couldn't be held beyond the next day on a

misdemeanor traffic violation. He was released on his own recognizance with a maximum bond of two hundred and fifty dollars.

CHAPTER TWENTY-FOUR

He stood at the sink and ate microwave spaghetti. He was naked except for the six-pointed star he wore on a gold chain. It was the trophy he snatched from Daddy's neck after he was killed. On the kitchen table, a note lay atop a newspaper article about Brian Rice.

The phone rang. Before he could finish 'hello,' the caller said, "He's going to run. You can't wait any longer." The voice commanded, "Do it now!"

He dumped the remainder of his dinner in the garbage then dressed and rechecked his work bag. He drove the black Toyota to a McDonald's drive thru.

#

Jeremy Butterworth winked at his reflection in the mirror and rubbed his hands over his shaved head and face. "Nothing like my mug shot!"

He stepped quietly into the bedroom and took the keys to his girlfriend's car. She remained asleep in a self-induced drugged stupor.

"Let the stupid bitch keep the van."

He filled boxes with tools and camping equipment, and stuffed clothes and food into plastic bags.

He carried the last box out and closed the trunk, returned to his trailer for a six-pack, and bounded for the car.

"I'm outta here."

A crushing blow came down on Jeremy's head. The beer dropped to the ground along with the keys.

#

Except for his boots and socks, Jeremy had been stripped; his hands taped behind him; his feet tied with rope; his body arched like a horseshoe.

The man in the baseball cap bent Jeremy's head back and crammed more pills down the dazed man throat. He struggled against his restraints but to no avail.

A rag was shoved deep into Jeremy's mouth. Duct tape sealed it in tight. Jeremy's eyes bulged as he choked on his vomit.

"Stay quiet, scumbag." He slammed the trunk lid closed with Jeremy stuffed inside, pulled the ball cap down, and got into the black Toyota. He was hungry. He remembered his uneaten spaghetti and reached for a hamburger from a bag on the seat.

Anxious to get to his destination, he drove north on US-19. Police lights flashed in his mirror. "Damn!" Flushed with fear, he did a mental check. No weapons; only my "karmic tool" in the trunk with the 'garbage.'

He pulled over and lowered the window. The Highway Patrol officer approached and asked for his license and registration. He handed it to the trooper and asked, "What did I do, sir? I'm sure I wasn't speeding."

"No, sir, you weren't, but your tail light is out."

Don't let him go to the back of the car! If the slug in there moves . . .

The trooper saw the half dozen McDonald's bags on the passenger seat and said, "You sure must be hungry."

"Naw, my son's having a sleep-over with his team," he said, with the sincere pride of a soccer dad. "I bought them for the boys."

"Okay, Sir. You'd better get those to the kids before they get cold. Be sure to get that light fixed in the morning."

"Yes, Officer." As he pulled away from the shoulder, a loud thump came from the trunk.

#

The bound and gagged man was dragged through the mud and swamp by the rope that tied his ankles together.

"Don't fight me, brother," said the man in the baseball cap. "This is your Karma."

At the embankment, the battered and cut, semi-conscious Jeremy was dragged into the water up to his shoulders. He squirmed.

"Stay put, Pervert!" He opened a can of beer and poured it ceremoniously over the mud-splashed man's head. He unwrapped the burgers and scattered them on the ground; removed a burlap sack from his duffel and staked the four corners of the bag, pinning Jeremy's head down in the muck.

He poked at the creep with his foot, then leaned over and spoke into his ear, "You must pay for your deeds ten times over."

Muffled cries came from under the burlap.

The captor tossed a pouch toward the bait. The child molester thrashed.

The man in the ball cap made sure to pick up the paper wrappers.

He pointed the flashlight at the water. Several pair of red eyes approached.

Halfway back to the car, he lingered until the churning water quieted and the chaos ended.

"Another win for the gators!"

#

Alerted by Jeremy's girlfriend, deputies arrived at the mobile home and found bags packed, hair in the sink, her car—its trunk loaded with boxes, a six pack and car keys on the ground; but no Jeremy Butterworth.

CHAPTER TWENTY-FIVE

On his way back from the swamp, the 'Chosen One' pulled into a twenty-four hour gas station that had an automatic car wash. He paid the cashier, pulled his car in, closed his eyes and listened to the water wash away the grime. He, too, felt himself being cleansed like a woman going to a mikvah.

By the time he arrived home, he was still pumped with adrenaline. He decided to clean out the trunk before he went to bed. It took a couple of hours to satisfy him that all traces of the pedophile were removed. He made a mental note to have the taillight fixed tomorrow.

In the shower, he rubbed his shoulder. The hot, steamy water relaxed his sore muscles. "That gator bait was heavier than I expected."

He crawled into bed and drifted off to sleep, sure that his immediate obedience would be acknowledged.

It hurts, Daddy! Stop! Please! His cries woke him. He lay in the bed and waited for the fear to subside.

Restless, he got out of bed, turned on the television and padded naked to the kitchen and gulped milk from the carton. He picked up the news clipping about the little boy that he had left on the table.

"Not to worry, Brian. The bastard didn't get away." With methodical precision, he folded the papers and put them in the file with the others.

He sat at the table and read yesterday's <u>Tampa Courier</u>. Appeals ran out for a man imprisoned twenty-six years for the rape and murder of a pregnant woman. The man was executed at midnight.

Twenty-six fucking years . . . our way is more efficient.

What he felt after his first mission hadn't returned. But, he received a modicum of satisfaction in the knowledge that there was a better way than the burdensome legal system. Someday ordinary citizens will see and praise the good that we do.

Rather than finish reading, he dropped the paper on top of the spaghetti container inside the trash can.

At his desk, he opened his journal and wrote:

Everyone benefits from our good works

1. Saving lives of the innocent.
2. Saving the taxpayers a shit-load of money for a trial, appeals, and for prison stays with all the benefits.
3. Allowing me to gain good Karma.
4. Freeing bastards from bad Karma.

"Dying in order to balance the scales is not an ending. It's a clean start! I am the 'Hand of Karma,' and I will reap the rewards for giving them a new beginning."

CHAPTER TWENTY-SIX

The holiday season had begun, but Allison wasn't in a holiday mood. She had accepted Kent's death. The intensity of her grief had faded. But, trepidation still remained over the matter of the police investigation.

She reminded herself to call Detective Massaro again for any updates, even though she knew he'd give her the same response. "We're working on it. We'll let you know when we know more." At this point, how can they believe she had anything to do with his death?

The research on the psychics Allison investigated consumed a good deal of her time, and if that wasn't sufficient, she'd committed to a library lecture series around the state. Then, there were the demands of Phillip who pressed her to do more than two shows a month. To that, she said no. It would slow her progress on the book she had to complete. A major publisher had seen her show and expressed an interest.

#

The sign read, 'World Famous Physic.' *Oh that's priceless! Now we're a laxative!* "What more could I ask?" Allison parked around the corner to prevent the reader from gleaning any information. She approached Madam Marie's storefront and was greeted by a neon sign of a hand with an eye in the palm. She shook her head.

A heavy-set young man with a gold-framed front tooth, smiled at her and held the door open, "Have a nice day," then, he exited. Inside, a diminutive, middle-aged woman, neatly attired in a plain cotton dress, greeted her.

"I'm Madam Marie," she said. "It's so nice to see you. Let me take your jacket and bag." Allison was disinclined to do so. "Don't be nervous, dear. I'll put them in the locker for you. You see, the reading room is sacred. You can't bring anything in there. It's where my spirits guide me."

A reluctant Allison agreed. "Oh, but can I please take notes? I'm so forgetful."

"All right, dear. I think the spirits will make an exception for that—but, no recording devices. It interferes with my connection to the unseen world."

Allison removed the notepad and pen from her purse. Madame Marie opened the locker and gestured to her.

"You see, it's empty. You're not to worry, dear. Everyone does it, and besides, it has a lock."

Allison hung her jacket on the hook and placed her purse on the shelf. The reader closed the door and locked it.

"Here, you hold this," and placed the key in Allison's hand. "Your things will be safe there."

With one hand holding back heavy gold curtains, Madame Marie asked Allison to be seated in the Reading Room, which was decorated with garish red, overstuffed, velvet furniture. The ornate lamp gave off minimum light. In the center of a round table, covered with a thick red velvet cloth, was a crystal ball. The walls were adorned with pictures of angels, saints, and Jesus. A huge crucifix hung over the doorway.

Madame Marie lit three white candles and turned off the lamp. She placed a finger to her lips, "Shhh." She lowered her head as if in prayer.

"The spirits are with me," she said in a low voice. "I can feel them gathering." She made circular motions with her hands over the crystal ball, started to chant-was it gibberish?-all the while she cleared her throat. The seer started to cough. "Please, excuse me, dear. Let me get a glass of water."

She returned a short time later and began the reading with the usual mundane statements: "you're sensitive, you're intelligent, you're caring," . . . and then, "I see you have a thyroid problem, but I believe you have it under control." Madame Marie posed as if she was honing in on a distant sound.

"Oh, dearie, you're such a giving and honest person. People take advantage of you all the time." She closed her eyes. "Oh, you're also a football fan." She cocked her head. "What's that, spirits?" Her eyes opened wide. "Oh yes, you follow the Buccaneers."

"Madame Marie, may I—"

"Hush, hush, dear. Let Madame Marie finish before my spirits leave me." She tilted her head. "Thank you, spirits." Her gaze locked on Allison's eyes. "I'm having difficulty understanding spirit. Do the initials 'CC' mean anything to you?"

"No."

"Are you sure? I see a big black bag and it's very special."

"Oh, yes." *My new Chanel bag.* "Now I remember," Allison replied.

"You see, Madame Marie does see all things." Without warning, she pushed back her chair. "Oh my goodness! This is terrible! The spirits tell me someone is trying to harm you!"

Allison put down her pen. She remembered the voice calling her name, 'Allison, Allison Rogers.'

"How fortunate you are," Madame Marie emphasized, "that you were guided to me today. Danger is imminent! There's a curse put on you by someone in contact with the dark forces. They're envious and near you."

Allison shifted in her chair.

"Don't fret, dear. Madame Marie can stop this evil before it goes any further. You must give me three hundred dollars."

"Did you say three hundred dollars?"

"Yes, dear, so Madame Marie can burn holy incense and special purple candles that are blessed to protect you. Madame Marie's gift has the force to halt this curse; and if you give me an extra hundred dollars, Madame Marie can turn this curse around and send it back to the evil one who wants to harm you. It's a rule of life, you get what you give. But I must start the prayers today."

"I'm so sorry," Allison spoke up. "I can't believe the time. I have to meet someone and I'm running late. I'll have to come back for the extra ceremony." Allison stood. "Besides, I don't have that kind of money with me."

"My, my, dearie. You know Madame Marie sees everything. I know you have three hundred dollars for the blessing ceremony!"

"As I said, I must go. I'll just get my belongings now."

"Remember my warning, dearie." The psychic was at her side and had hold of her hand before Allison could leave the room. "Be sure to bring the three hundred dollars to me today, before sunset and the extra one hundred dollars if you want to send it back to the jealous one."

"Thank you, Madame Marie. I promise I won't forget."

Allison went to the cabinet. She opened the locked door. Her jacket had fallen from the hook and was placed neatly on top of her purse.

#

He was about to leave his office when his desk phone rang. "Detective DeMarcou."

"Hi, Steve. This is Allison Rogers. Do you have a minute?"

"For you? Sure."

"You're familiar with the research I do for my show?"

"Uh huh."

"I thought I'd ask you for some advice. I need to keep my

identity concealed until I finish my story, but, I'm so angry . . . I'd like to know if I have grounds to file a complaint."

"Why don't you tell me what happened and we'll go from there."

Comforted by the tone in his voice, Allison relaxed and repeated the events of her reading with Madame Marie and how she suspected someone got into her purse even though it was locked away.

"Steve, she had to know about the medicine I take because the prescription was in my pocketbook, along with the receipt for the Chanel bag I ordered!"

"What kind of bag?"

"It doesn't matter, it's a girl thing." *A girl thing, Allison?* "That's how Madame Marie knew so much. When I got to my car, I checked my purse. That's when I discovered the tickets for the Bucs game this weekend were gone. And, they were club seats! Emma's gonna kill me."

"If you lost my club tickets, I might do it myself!"

"Very funny." Her mood lightened.

"Anything else missing?"

She informed him that she had a bank envelope with three hundred and twenty dollars in it but when she checked it, the three hundred was there, but the twenty dollar bill was gone.

"At first I wanted to go back in, but I thought it more prudent to leave."

"Good decision. Let me talk to O'Keefe. He's a friend of mine and a big fan of yours. Can I call you later?"

"Thanks. I'd be grateful."

#

"Emma, I'm so sorry about the tickets! I can't believe she got the best of me."

"Drink your wine. It'll help you calm down."

"Forget calming down. I know what I'm going to do. I'll call Phillip at the T.V. station first thing in the morning. I want to move the report on the 'world famous physic' up to this week.

She swallowed the last mouthful of red wine and splashed some onto her white silk blouse. "Oh, great! The perfect end to a perfect day," she said, dabbing at the stain. "I hope the cretin who stole the tickets will be stupid enough to sit in our seats!"

"We can only hope," Emma said, with exasperation.

CHAPTER TWENTY-SEVEN

In the outer waiting room that was appointed with leather chairs and marble tables, Allison double-checked her wallet to make sure she had placed the two hundred dollars there for her reading with Anne Preston. She heard muffled voices of people who approached from the inner office. The man's voice sounded belligerent. Now closer to the door, a woman spoke.

"You're right, Mr. Keller. I didn't tell you what you expected, but I did tell you the truth."

The man closed the office door behind him with a deliberate yank and hurried through the waiting room.

Allison read him for an instant as he passed. She knew he had, indeed, heard the truth.

The door re-opened. An attractive redhead, with the most beautiful green eyes Allison had ever seen, greeted her in a calm and gentle tone.

"Hello. I'm Anne Preston. Please do come in."

"And, I'm Martha Baker." Allison took a seat across the desk from the psychic. "Isn't that patchouli I smell?"

"Yes. I've always found it soothing."

"Oh! What a beautiful paperweight. Baccarat Crystal?" Allison leaned forward to touch it. "May I?"

"I'm sorry," Anne said, moving the paperweight out of Allison's reach. "It was given to me by a member of the Royal Family. I prefer no one touch it. As a matter of fact, no one has handled the crystal since I first acquired it. It radiates an energy that comforts me."

Allison attempted to read Anne.

Anne blinked a couple of times and a slight smile appeared.

"Let's begin, shall we?" Anne reached across the desk and touched Allison's hand. "What a frightful year this has been for you. The infidelity in your marriage; and then your husband's death, could only be devastating!"

Allison's eyes widened.

"Are you all right, Mrs. Baker? Do you need some time?"

"No. I'm fine," answered Allison.

"Shall we go on, then?"

Allison nodded.

The reading was complete with generalities about Allison's family, education, and childhood.

"Now let's move forward. You recently met a man who had romantic potential. Another place, another time it might have worked. I have suffered with that feeling myself. I've never had a lasting relationship. But that's often the burden of an intuitive." She took a sip of water. "And, this man is quite attractive."

Anne stopped speaking and placed her hand on the crystal.

"You've taken on a new job. Most people wouldn't understand your need to submerse yourself in your work so soon after the tribulations you've been through, but I do. I'm sure you know you have more trials to face. As you usually do, you'll land on your feet. However, I must caution you. The project you've taken on could put you in harm's way! I suggest you trust your intuition. It's usually right, Mrs. Baker—or, may I call you Mrs. Rogers?"

Allison's cheeks reddened.

"That wasn't a psychic observation, Mrs. Rogers. I have seen you on the telly." Anne winked.

"Ms. Preston, I'm sure you understand that I had to come

incognito." She reached for her wallet, but Anne stopped her.

"That won't be necessary. Please consider this session a professional courtesy; one psychic to another."

Alone in her office, Anne held the crystal and gazed out of the window.

"Allison Rogers, you're intelligent, nosey, and tenacious. I don't care to see you again, but I trust, I will."

#

Intrigued by Anne's reading, Allison was excited to share with her sister what she had learned and her embarrassment when her cover as Martha Baker was exposed.

"Funny, by the way everyone spoke about her, I expected someone much older. I'll give her credit, she's good. Not everything she said was specific, but she did bring up Kent, about when Dad left, and Grand-dad's hand-carved chess set."

"I'm waiting for the 'but'," Emma said.

"She sure didn't want me reading her. The minute I tried, a strong wall of energy went up around her. And that English accent—so affected."

CHAPTER TWENTY-EIGHT

From the time five-year-old Anne was in her first foster home, she saw things no one else could see, things she didn't always understand. Naomi and Don Hall, her foster parents, were deeply religious and kind, but displayed affection only toward their own child, Wynette.

Annie and Wynette went to Sunday school while the adults attended church services. One Easter Sunday, Annie blurted out to her Sunday school teacher, Miss Boody, that she could see and talk to angels like Jesus and that the angels told her to tell grownups what they said. Just like the prophets in the Bible.

"Annie!" Miss Boody gasped. "You must never tell a lie like that again. Now, apologize!"

"Why? I'm not lying. You told me lying is bad." Her lip quivered. "The angels told me you have a baby in your belly and your mom's gonna make you go away. I don't want you to go away, Miss Boody! I love you."

She tugged at Annie's arm, ushered her out to the hall, and scolded her for saying something so terrible. Annie cried. Miss Boody made her sit on a wooden bench outside the classroom door to wait for Naomi and Don who were horrified by Annie's remarks.

"Only someone bad would say those things, Annie!" Don barked at her. "You must be punished. You'll stay in your room til tomorrow—and not have any supper!"

By summertime, the Hall's were frightened when Annie was proven right. Miss Boody was pregnant and was asked to quit teaching Sunday school. In the months that followed, Annie told the Hall's the car was going to break down on the way to church, and it did! She said Wynette would fall and break her arm the day before it happened. The angels told her Daddy Don would get fired and a week later he lost his job.

Naomi was convinced Annie made these things happen and was in league with the devil.

No matter how many times Annie was punished for telling about the visions, she continued.

"But, the angels tell me—"

"Shut your mouth, child! Angels wouldn't talk to YOU!"

The last straw came when Annie said they couldn't go to church this week because Daddy Don would be in the hospital. Three days later Don fell at his new job and broke his foot so severely he had to have surgery.

Annie was once again punished for the demons that were in her. She sat alone in the small closet where she had to stay until she confessed to being bad.

Daddy Don came to let her out of the closet to use the bathroom. Skippy, the family dog was at his feet. Annie saw the dog was going to die soon, so, when Daddy Don forced her back into the dark space, an enraged Annie screamed at him.

"I'm going to make Skippy die if you don't let me out of here!"

"You evil child! He hasn't done anything to you! Now you'll stay in there even longer!"

Later that week, Naomi took Skippy for his evening walk. The dog broke free of his leash and ran out in front of a truck.

Sick with fear that Annie was possessed, the Hall's contacted the church elders to perform an exorcism.

"Angels do talk to me; it's not the devil!" Annie screamed in defiance.

The Department of Child Services was alerted to the extreme ordeal the Halls had permitted. Annie was placed with another foster family. Even with the harsh treatment forced upon her by the Halls, Annie didn't stop 'seeing.' But, she did stop telling.

For Anne, 'seeing' became a secret tool she used to protect herself from the others who didn't have her power.

CHAPTER TWENTY-NINE

He opened the garage door and parked next to his Jaguar convertible. The last time he drove it was Thanksgiving. He adjusted its dust cover and picked up a crumpled MacDonald's burger wrapper off the floor. It had been overlooked when he was finished with Butterworth.

Inside the kitchen, he turned on the small television, went to the bar in the living room and poured himself a drink. He almost quit his job today after the shit he got from his boss for coming in late. He dropped his clothes on the floor in a heap and sat naked in the dark. The only illumination in the room came from the TV in the kitchen. He downed the scotch and poured another. His old nemesis, depression, came at him from behind like a monster from the mist. He rubbed his temples.

A game of computer Solitaire would distract him. He played for awhile and emptied the liquor bottle. This time it didn't work. No amount of alcohol, or the game, could keep the demon from swallowing him.

Without warning, the image of his father's face replaced the card game on the screen. He pulled his hand away from the mouse as if zapped by a bolt of electricity. The voice repeated, "You will never escape what you've done. You must make retribution for your sins."

He slapped his hand over the mouth on the screen, but couldn't silence the voice.

Daddy closed and locked the door. Something was different about him. Daddy made a scary smile and unbuckled his belt. His pants fell down. Daddy rubbed himself up and down and it got bigger and bigger.

Daddy grabbed my hand and put it there. "This feels funny Daddy."

"Sheldon! What's going on in there?"

"Just a minute, Deborah," Daddy pulled up his pants. "Bad boy!" he shouted. "Don't you ever do that again!"

He slapped my face.

Daddy opened the bathroom door and Mommy just stood there and cried. "It's okay Deborah. Our little boy had to learn a lesson that when you do bad things you must pay ten times over."

What did I do wrong? What did I do wrong?

It took four fucking years to perfect my plan so no one would ever suspect the son of the Perfect Family. He grinned, and remembered that first blow to Daddy's face, shattering his teeth. How many years did he think he could use me for his deviant pleasure? I hope he knew it was the same golf club he used to rape me.

Dad had to die first. Mom was used to standing by. She pretended she didn't know. She was next.

The police said they'd been 'robbed and murdered.' How fortuitous. Any more perfect and it would have appeared planned!

From the time he entered high school, he fantasized about ways to kill his parents. By the start of his senior year, his plan was in place. He'd ask a classmate who he knew wouldn't accept his invitation, to go camping with him. He'd take the ten hour drive to the Suwannee River in Live Oak, FL and set up camp. He'd make sure to frequent the town's stores and get receipts for his supplies. On the 'chosen day,' he'd stop for an early dinner at the local restaurant then drive to 'see' his parents. He had found the ideal spot to bury the small metal box of valuables he would take from the house—it had to look like a robbery. He'd let it sit for a year before he'd retrieve it. He'd make it back to the campsite by late afternoon, clean up, and would be sure to have a dinner at the same restaurant – leaving with a receipt.

His parents wouldn't be found for days. No one would miss them until they didn't show up for their Bridge game. He had plenty of time to rehearse his 'shock' at the news of the death of his 'perfect parents.'

I could have won an Oscar! A perfect performance. Ancient history.

#

The digital clock displayed ten thirty. "Shit!" He'd overslept. "Fuck it. I'll call in sick."

He turned over, reached under his pillow and stroked the book—his special gift from her.

"Mine to give, yours to keep, only the two of us know; that special place between two souls, where only we can go."

How my life changed since we met. My first reading was a test to see if anyone could see what happened to my most deserving parents.

They'd never prove it anyway.

How'd he ever get so lucky to know such a spiritual and important lady? She must have seen a good spot on his soul to mentor him in the ways of retribution.

She understood what he had done and why. She saw the abused little boy who tried to be good and not make trouble. She never judged him. She knew about his evil father and how Mom always protected Dad. She knew the pain he'd suffered.

"How'd she know so much? She's amazing!"

He trusted her and liked the way their eyes met when she read him. He enjoyed the warmth of her touch when she placed her hand on his to comfort him when he felt pain. He wondered if it meant as much to her.

She told him his tortured soul would never stop suffering until he fulfilled his Karma. She declared that he didn't have to be a victim. He could become an advocate. Killing his parents wasn't sufficient to satisfy his Karma. She made it sound so normal—"make those pay who think they got away and your karmic debt will be re-paid."

"It's remarkable how good I am at my new vocation and she's just begun to teach me."

He opened the secretary desk, filled his fountain pen and began to write.

> *Dear Mom and Dad,*
> *I've sent you two more friends. You have much in common. One is the real McCoy; the other is a Gator's fan.*
>
> > *Your Son,*
> > *The Teacher's Pet*

CHAPTER THIRTY

The volume of messages that came into the station for her never ceased to amaze Allison. Included in this week's stack of mail that she brought home was a note from a woman who claimed to be a 'bona fide' psychic. Her name is 'Veejay.' She professed to be a seventh generation intuitive.

Allison scheduled a meeting for the next week.

Calls out of the way, she went out to the pool and sat in the lounge. She closed her eyes and started to drift off. Thoughts of Steve interrupted her rest.

"What is wrong with me? He's a cop and unbelievably aggravating!" she said, aloud. She had no idea why she was so drawn to him, but she couldn't deny the chemistry.

She was deep in thought when the phone rang.

"Hi, Allison. It's Steve DeMarcou. I wanted to bring you up to speed on that complaint you asked about. We arrested a guy who tried to sell your football tickets. Get this—turns out he's the son of that psychic, Madame Marie! He threw his mother under the bus and confessed to it all. They worked their scam together. While Mom put on her performance, the son used an extra key to the locker. He went through the customer's belongings; got all kinds of information. When Mom excused herself from the 'mark,' he'd pass on what he found to her. It's quite a racket. They've both been arrested and their place shut down."

"Now I'm glad he took the tickets. I've got a good ending to my report for Channel Six and a new chapter for my book. It would be great if I could consult with some of their other victims."

"Right now, you're the only one who owns up to being taken by these losers. Nobody else will admit they've been conned. That's how these people get away with it. So you know, they bonded out, but I doubt they'll be back in business anytime soon."

"Thanks for letting me know, Steve."

"No problem. Now, try to stay out of trouble."

She smiled at the concern in his voice.

#

With her keys in hand, she approached her car. The street light under which Allison had parked had gone out. She surveyed the area around her vehicle and sensed something off kilter. *You just had to shop til they closed. Couldn't pass up that sale.* The hackles on the back of her neck stood up. A threatening presence.

She pressed the remote, opened the door, and threw her packages across the seat; her purse hit the passenger door, and spilled onto the floor.

Close to panic, she locked the doors and started the engine. A figure in dark clothes jumped out of the bushes in front of her car and lunged toward the driver side door for the handle. Allison laid on the horn and slammed the car into gear. The man took off. He ran into the stand of trees on the far side of the deserted parking lot. The tires screeched as she pulled onto the road.

Allison burst through the front door breathless and trembling. "Emma, where are you?" she yelled. "I just had the scare of my life!"

Emma hurried into the room.

Allison blurted out, "He scared the hell out of me!" and recounted the incident.

"My God, Allison! Are you hurt?"

"No, just rattled."

"Did you report it?"

"Of course, I did! My phone was somewhere on the floor, so I drove straight to the police station. I didn't see the guy's face so I don't know how much good that will do." She massaged the back of her neck.

"Wait a minute! Remember the warnings that Preston woman and that astrologer gave me? Do you think this is what they meant? They both mentioned danger and for me to be aware of my surroundings."

"All I can say is you were lucky, little sister. You could have been hurt, or worse. He could have stolen your new Chanel bag!" Emma's joke broke the tension.

#

Allison put the incident at the mall last week behind her, but occasional thoughts of what could have been still rattled her. Determined to get back to work, she confirmed her appointment with Veejay-the seventh generation psychic.

Allison allowed a little extra time to walk the length of the boardwalk at John's Pass; a sleepy little shopping village frequented by tourists. The sound of the gulls and the smell of the Gulf of Mexico filled her with a sense of wellbeing. She stood alongside tourists who leaned against the rail watching dolphin make their way through the pass and back out into the blue-green waters of the Gulf.

The small stores and walkways were packed with seasonal visitors who shopped for seashell treasures or handmade 'somethings' to take home with them. Allison bought a gelato and sat at a vacant table, people-watching, and savored the peaceful beauty around her.

She turned and saw a young man on bended knee, proposing to a pretty young woman.

Allison was reluctant to leave the tranquility but she didn't want to be late.

The shop blended in with the quaint design of John's Pass retail stores. Allison was welcomed by a beautiful young woman who wore a sari and sindoor bindi.

"Hello. You are, Allison Rogers?" The woman flipped her waist-length black hair over her shoulder. "You're right on time. I'm Veejay." Her dark eyes were penetrating.

"I am so happy you agreed to do this interview, Veejay."

"No, it is my honor." She motioned for Allison to sit.

"Veejay—that's an interesting name."

"It's really a nickname. The Indian version is too long and difficult for Americans to pronounce."

Allison turned on her recorder. "Your message indicated you are a seventh generation psychic. I'd like to know more about your background."

"Well, my family is from India, but I was born here."

"That would explain why you have no distinct accent."

"Oh. I get asked about that a lot." Veejay pointed to the bindi. "And this dot, too. But, it's our family's tradition."

Allison smiled at Veejay's reference to the 'dot' on her forehead.

"What can you tell me about your psychic abilities, Veejay?"

"First, would you care for a cup of Chai tea?"

"No thanks. I'm enjoying our conversation."

"Our abilities, as you call them, seem to run only in the females in my family. We're mostly born gifted. We can see the past, present, and future. Of course, we have to handle these gifts with utmost respect and seriousness. I'm sure you know that."

For twenty minutes Allison was bombarded by Veejay's tall tales of how she had 'anonymously' helped solve every major crime in the United States over the last ten years by using her skills, and how she'd 'never' consider taking any credit for it.

"Really?" Allison raised an eyebrow. Oh, great! Another bona fide '*physic*.' She cleared her throat. "You spoke earlier of your family tradition of wearing the bindi."

Veejay seemed confused.

"The dot on your head—can you tell me if the color has any bearing on what you do as a seer, or is it more of a religious symbol?"

Veejay's face lit up, her finger pointed to her forehead. "It's more of a tribal thing."

"I believe I have a clear picture," Allison retorted. "So, the bindi identifies your family members, or even people of your own faith, or sect?"

"That's right," answered Veejay.

"Then, you're people are Hindu."

"Oh, no, we're from the Sioux tribe."

Sioux? "I think that's all I need for now. Thank you, Veejay."

That was a first; a Native American wearing a sari. What's next; an Inuit wearing a grass skirt?

#

The nail salon was quieter than usual. Allison closed her eyes and relaxed while the manicurist worked. She thought about her upcoming segment and didn't want to feature another negative spin—Veejay would be . . . she almost laughed at the thought. She imagined the impact of a psychic of Anne Preston's caliber appearing on her show. She speculated that if Anne would agree, it would be a dramatic contrast to the fiasco with Veejay; but, if Anne Preston claims she's a blood relative to Cleopatra, Allison would consider a new career.

Filled with anticipation of a live interview with Anne, Allison dialed the psychic's office before she left the shop. ". . . I'll see you Thursday."

#

"Mrs. Rogers, you were somewhat vague when we spoke. What

is it you would like to discuss with me?"

Allison pitched her idea. Before she could finish—

"I find you a delightful person and I believe it is a stellar service you are attempting to provide to the community, however, I do not do interviews." Anne pressed her hands flat on the desk. "I recognize your flattery. But, if you will excuse me . . ."

Refusing her perfunctory dismissal, Allison pleaded, "May I have a minute more, for a few general inquiries?" She didn't wait for a response. "For instance, where were you born? How long have you been here? Are there other psychics in your family?"

Anne stood, "Mrs. Rogers, this is unacceptable. I do not give interviews. But I will give you a piece of advice. Be more careful with the people you investigate. This work can attract harmful elements. I suggest you take extra precautions. Danger can be right in front of you and you best see it!"

A perturbed Allison was ushered to the door.

"Well, wasn't that a bite in the asp!" Allison huffed.

CHAPTER THIRTY-ONE

Allison had loved stormy days from the time she was a little girl. Today the rain brought memories of the old farm house kitchen in Ohio and how safe and secure she felt then. She could almost smell the aroma of fresh baked bread and hearty vegetable soup Mom made.

Comfortable in her jammies, she sat at her computer. Her intent was to work on her manuscript. She rummaged through papers that were scattered around her desk but stopped when the garage door opened. Emma had returned from her reading with Anne Preston.

"Emma, how'd it go?"

"It was a cinch driving in this treacherous rain. Thanks for asking." Thunder shook the windows. "The next time you send me out to play Nancy Drew, ask me why I volunteered to help with your investigations."

In the kitchen, Emma opened the tin of Molasses snaps and made tea. Allison reached for a cookie.

"So, tell me what happened?"

"You were right about her being a good reader. She does come across sincere. She started with the usual pleasantries; but, that's a phony accent if I ever heard one! Most of what she told me was accurate, like I was kind and generous, brilliant and creative, and did I mention, humble?"

"I think I need that cup of tea now!" Allison reached for the teapot. "Did she know you were psychic?"

"She didn't mention it. She did reveal events and characteristics about Harry that I hadn't thought about for years. What I found odd was that she never mentioned I had a sister.

Allison, didn't she tell you she's never had a lasting relationship?"

"Yeah. Why?"

"After she talked about Harry and how fortunate I was to have had such a good marriage, she told me she was a widow who had been married for twenty years, and that she too had lost her wonderful husband to a coronary embolism!"

"She said what? That's bizarre."

"And, get this," Emma stirred her tea, "she said her husband's name was Harry!"

A flash of lightning and clap of thunder shook the house. Emma got up and drew the drapes.

"Why would she lie about that?" Allison asked.

"Maybe she just wants to identify with her clients."

"That's a possibility."

"By the way, Allison, have you found anything about her on the internet?"

"Nothing."

CHAPTER THIRTY-TWO

A Sheriff's Office spokesman, Alex Curtis, reported during the televised press conference, that two third-graders discovered a body on the playground of the Wazalis Academy in Hillsborough County. The beaten body was identified as that of Wayne Bailey, a known drug dealer. Bailey was released from prison last month after serving time for possession of child pornography.

Witnesses reported seeing a dark colored Toyota at two-thirty this morning, pulling away from where the body was later found.

"Big fucking deal! There are a million Toyotas around here." When the press conference ended he turned off the television, creased the note in half, and placed it in the file with the others.

CHAPTER THIRTY-THREE

Wrapped in a robe, Allison had just finished drying her hair when the phone rang.

"Hello, Allison. This is Detective DeMar—, Steve DeMarcou."

"Hi," butterflies fluttered in her stomach, "what can I do for you?"

"There's something I'd like to talk to you about. Can I stop by?"

He arrived an hour later, Allison heard him laugh when the doorbell chimes played Take Me Out To The Ballgame.

She invited him in and watched as he scanned the room. "Nice house," Steve said, as he followed her into the sunroom.

"My sister and her husband had it built years ago. It was their dream home."

He walked straight to the game table. "Allison, this is incredible," and picked up a chess piece. "Do you play?"

"As a matter of fact, both Emma and I were taught to play on that very set. Our grand-dad carved it."

"These pieces are amazing!"

"And so was grand-dad." She motioned for him to take a seat. "So what did you want to talk about?"

"I'd like you to clarify something you said the night we met about the crime that happened near Tropicana Field."

She tried to hide the disappointment she felt when she realized this was a business visit.

"I want you to know upfront, I don't believe in this psychic stuff. But seeing how you dabble in it I thought—"

"Dabble? You said, dabble?" *How can he be so handsome and be such an ass?*

"Bad choice of words. There were some colored stones found at another crime scene."

"Is this about the guy beaten to death in Tampa?"

"And you're curious . . . why?" He sounded defensive.

"Don't look so astonished. After I read in the paper about the violent attack it made me think of the incident at Tropicana Field. I put two and two together. Almost got you, didn't I?" She had no intention of telling him she had picked it up psychically.

"The reason I'm here is," he handed her an 8x10 glossy. "I need . . . I mean . . . I want to know if you psychic-type people put any significance to these stones." He looked like he'd rather be having a colonoscopy instead of asking for her help. He said, "You do understand that all of this has to be kept confidential."

"Steve, I've worked with law enforcement before. I know the drill." With the photo in hand, she studied the picture. She felt Steve's misgivings.

"You have any idea what those mean?" He turned on the recorder.

"There's a belief that stones and crystals radiate different qualities of energy. This one is a black tourmaline. It's believed to absorb negativity." She pointed at the picture. "This is pink quartz. It's used for healing the heart energy; for instance, the pain of a bad relationship." *Wouldn't hurt him to carry one.*

"What about this one?" he asked, his hand brushing over hers as he pointed to the blue stone.

She responded to his intentional gesture with a slight smile. "It's lapis lazuli. The ancient Egyptians would pulverize it and apply the powder around their eyes to ward off evil spirits." She handed the photo back to him. "That's it in a nutshell."

He turned off the recorder and started to ask another question. Instead, he tucked the photograph into his pocket. "Thanks for the info. I'll pass it along."

"You've made it quite clear that you don't put much value in this 'psychic stuff' Steve, but what if the killer does? Suppose he believes these stones are aiding him. Maybe he's trying to release his own demons. It could be that he's completely indifferent to the victim." She waited for Steve's reply, but there was none. She saw only a Doubting Thomas. "Just a little food for thought."

CHAPTER THIRTY-FOUR

A reporter from the <u>Tampa Courier,</u> Octavine Diana, contacted Allison. "I've been following your Channel Six reports on psychic scams and would like to discuss something with you for a feature article that I am writing."

\#

The next morning when the reporter arrived, Allison greeted a woman whom she thought young enough to pass for a high school student. But, when the questions began, she knew Octavine Diana was an experienced reporter. "I'm aware of what happened in California, Mrs. Rogers. I'm sorry for your loss."

Allison hoped she wouldn't regret having this dialogue with Ms. Diana.

The two women discussed the different aspects of metaphysics and why, if people with heightened perceptions are so tuned in to the cosmos, can't they avoid problems in their own lives.

". . . I can't speak for everyone with ESP, but as a general rule, once an intuitive becomes emotionally involved, the rational mind takes over."

". . . My intention was to write a book about psychics and the good they can do. After I learned my favorite aunt had been duped out of thousands of dollars by a charlatan posing as a spiritual advisor, my objective changed."

Octavine pressed for more examples of swindles.

"A wealthy woman in Miami was convinced by a fake psychic that the reason her husband left her for a younger woman was that there was a curse on her money. He instructed her to bring in five, new, one hundred dollar bills. She did so. He proceeded to wrap the money in black tissue paper. After a slight of hand switch he had the woman set the package on fire to rid her of the curse. A week later, she repeated the ceremony with another five hundred dollars to ensure 'greater happiness' for her future. Not long after, the man was caught making the switch by an undercover police officer who posed as a grieving husband. The man was arrested.

"But, his arrest was too late for another elderly woman who gave him six thousand dollars over the course of a year, to break the curse that caused her adult son's addiction. After her son murdered a man during a drug-fueled rage, she committed suicide."

"I saw that report last year," Octavine said. "How can people be so gullible?"

"Gullible may not be the right word. These people are desperate for something. That's what makes it so easy for snake oil salesmen to prosper. They find out what that 'something' is and exploit it." Allison told the reporter about a self-proclaimed lottery psychic who claimed to have picked winning numbers for more than one hundred people.

"By the condition of her house and poor neglected dogs in the yard," Allison quipped, "she should have picked the winning numbers for herself."

At the conclusion of the interview, Octavine asked for a name or two of psychics with whom she could meet. Once outside of Allison's house, she opened the note with names and numbers: Sue Figgit/astrologer, Charles Colombo/clairvoyant, Anne Preston/psychic.

#

The day was pleasant and bright. The forecast was eighty degrees. Allison decided to walk to the fruit stand and found herself lost in thoughts of Steve. Her cell vibrated in her pocket. She was unable to make out the caller ID in the bright daylight.

"Hello?"

"You sent a reporter," the caller barked. "I told you I do not do interviews!"

"But I—"

"Mind your own affairs, Mrs. Rogers. You would be wise to keep your meddling nose out of my business!"

The dial tone let Allison know their conversation was over.

CHAPTER THIRTY-FIVE

According to his website, Charles Gabriel was a "World Renowned" reader and advisor to presidents, royalty, celebrities, and international police departments.

Allison parked beside a Mercedes sedan with the initials C G on the vanity plate. In her usual wig and glasses, she went inside.

"Hi, I'm Martha Baker. I'm scheduled at four o'clock," she said to the young blonde receptionist who seemed more interested in searching through her canvas shoulder bag than to what Allison was saying to her.

Allison moved to the seating area where she inspected the black and white publicity shots of celebrities on the wall. There were words of praise for Charles' accomplishments on each photo. However, the handwriting and the autographs were far too similar.

"How lucky you are to meet all of these famous people!" 'Martha' gushed to Laura Jobes, Mr. Gabriel's secretary.

"Oh, the photographs were here when I came to work for Mr. Gabriel last year."

The door on the far side of the office opened.

"Miss Baker," he drawled with the charm of a southern gentleman, "come on in and make yourself comfortable."

When they shook hands she caught him gawking at her breasts. He lifted his gaze to meet her eyes. His broad smile framed oversized capped teeth. His face was void of emotion. Heavy-lidded eyes lowered again to her chest. His behavior was vulgar.

He began with a nonspecific reading. Despite the fact that his fascination with her breasts made her uneasy, she remained in character.

"Mr. Gabriel, may I ask how long you've been doing this work? You must have been born psychic."

"Yes," he boasted. "I was blessed with the gift of second sight."

"I have to admit I read about you on the internet." She showed him a disarming smile. "You must be absolutely wonderful to have so many famous people as followers. That's why I came to see you."

"Yes, I do have a loyal following, Martha." He smoothed his hair back. "Darlin', you flatter me too much. What say we take care of your reading first and then we can visit properly. I sense you are interested in more than a reading from me . . . something personal." He winked.

"Mr. Gabriel, I sense you are VERY mistaken." Anger brought her out of character. "May I ask you a question?" Not waiting for his permission, "What presidents have you advised? Did you work for Interpol or Scotland Yard? According to your website—"

His expression made the hairs on the back of her neck stand up. "Oh, I know who you are!" He started around the desk toward her. "You're that arrogant woman I saw on the television."

He took another step.

Allison was alarmed by the controlled rage on his face and knew the violence that hid beneath the surface. "Stop right there!" Frightened, she moved to the door.

"Little lady, if you think you're gonna make a fool outta me, you've got another think coming!" He swallowed hard. "You'd best get out of here Missy or I won't be held responsible."

She raced past the receptionist who watched with wide eyes and open mouth.

From the doorway, his voice boomed, "And, you'd better not mention my name on one of your television shows or you won't like what happens. I'm not someone you want to mess with."

"Should I take that as a threat, Mr. Gabriel?" She knew wasn't posturing.

"Read into it whatever you want, little lady."

At the door, she reached into her pocket, lifted the recorder for him to see, and winked. She hadn't broken the law and recorded him without his permission because the recorder was off. But he didn't know that.

Upon her return home, there was a message from Laura Jobes who wanted to make sure Allison was safe. She was afraid that Mr. Gabriel was going to hurt her when he stormed out right after she left. Before she quit, she made a list of some of the people who came to see her former boss and thought Allison might discover some interesting facts for her show. Laura left her number for Allison.

#

At the end of the cobblestone driveway stood an English Tudor mansion. Allison knocked at the front door.

"Mrs. Rogers, I'm so happy you want to talk to me about Mr. Gabriel!" Mrs. Abbott fluffed her over-processed hair. "I thought we might be on camera."

"No. Not today," Allison said, as she sat on the sofa next to the excited woman who held her Siamese cat, Quan Yin. Allison asked, "Do I have your permission to record our conversation?"

The woman lifted her cat Quan Yin, and nuzzled it nose to nose. She asked Quan Yin in baby talk if it was okay with her. She told Allison Quan Yin was her little girl and best friend. "We're fine with recording. Quan Yin loves Mr. Gabriel, too."

After the glowing reference for the 'psychic to the stars' Mrs. Abbott couldn't give Allison any specific events that had come to pass as they were all predictions for the far future. She confessed that her husband thinks that she's a 'silly goose' for believing in Charles Gabriel.

"I swear he can see into my soul! Isn't that right, Quan Yin?" she petted the feline.

Allison turned off the recorder.

Mrs. Abbott leaned in to her. "There was an instant, I think we had some chemistry going, but he's too much of a gentleman to say anything. After all, I am married."

Allison left the mansion full of compassion for the woman who had so much in her life, and yet, nothing at all.

The next three people Allison spoke with did not have the same high regard for Charles Gabriel.

A further investigation of Charles Gabriel revealed that over a number of years he targeted unattached, wealthy women who came to consult with him. He professed his love to them, convinced them to open a joint bank account, to invest in his business ventures, and promised a return on their money, which never happened. Out of embarrassment, the women involved did not press charges.

Two of the women did agree to tell their story live during Allison's show as long as their identities were concealed.

CHAPTER THIRTY-SIX

Allison made a quick stop at the nail salon before she went to the station. She waited at the front counter and overheard a woman whisper to another patron, "Isn't that the know-it-all on TV who makes people who go to psychics out to be fools? I've been going to psychics for years and I'm no fool! Who is she to judge?" The woman looked Allison up and down as she took a seat next to her.

In a voice too loud to be ignored, Allison overheard the customer say:

"The one I go to is exceptional, and British, I think. She's expensive! Not everyone can afford her, but you know me, Kim!" The boisterous woman showed her nail tech a pouch from which she dumped three shiny stones onto the table. The leather pouch smelled of patchouli.

"She gave me these so that I can get what I want when I get that cheating son-of-a-bitch-husband-of-mine in court!" She dropped the stones back into the pouch. "The psychic said she used these exact stones through her own divorce and made out great! That's all I needed to hear!"

"Excuse me," Allison interrupted, "I couldn't help but overhear you mention a psychic. My name is Allison, and I was wondering if you would give me her name?"

"I was having a private conversation," the woman scolded. "I apologize if you thought I was speaking to YOU!" The woman left a tip on the table and walked away.

Allison's face turned beet red as all heads turned in her direction.

CHAPTER THIRTY-SEVEN

Los Angeles County, California

"Whatcha got for me?" Massaro asked Detective Lily Totah when she entered the room.

She removed her jacket and tossed it on a chair. "We know that Dominguez killed Kent Rogers, ballistics proved that. And, we've cleared everyone else including Kent's boyfriend, Fernando Diez. I know his fortune teller wife is involved! I can feel it."

"Hold on, Swami. Let's see what you found before I cross your palm with silver, okay?"

"Boss," she said, "I searched phone records for Dominguez and Mrs. Rogers. Found calls to her house, cell, and her work. There were eleven calls made within two weeks from Dominguez' home to Mrs. Rogers. Each call lasted less than a minute. And, they came in after Mrs. Dominguez moved out, so let's assume it wasn't her calling."

Detective Massaro tapped his pencil and asked, "What about a money trail?"

"I checked his bank accounts for recent deposits. The schlub was flat broke. I checked his wife's bank records for trust funds; off shore accounts; anything new or suspicious. Didn't find shit!" Totah took the pencil from Massaro's hand. "Must you do that?" She continued, "You gotta figure Rogers would pay Dominguez in cash. He probably gave his wife the money and she's holding on to it. I'm on to something."

"We're going to need more than that, Lily." Massaro poured two cups of coffee and handed her one. "I don't know if I should give you this. You're pretty wired already."

"Humor me for a minute." She added three packets of sugar to the cup. "Let's just say she hires Dominguez, then, she trashes her office. Makes it like someone broke in. When she and Dominguez have it all set, she closes up shop and moves to Florida. Neat and tidy."

"It's a start," Massaro said. "But we still need more."

"Then there's the sister-in-law, Emma." Totah added another sugar to her coffee. "Maybe she paid Dominguez. There wasn't any love lost between her and the vic. Christ knows she's got plenty of money and wouldn't miss it. It's a fact that the sisters are pretty tight. It might make her feel good to help her kid sister out of a bad marriage." Totah slurped the last of her coffee and poured another. "Look Boss, I need a little more time. I want to go back further into Allison Rogers' financials. We know her husband cheated on her from the time they got married. She probably planned on blowing his balls off for years."

CHAPTER THIRTY-EIGHT

Pinellas County, Florida

As was his normal routine, he undressed and turned on the television as soon as he walked through the door. The drone of voices made him feel less alone. His compulsion to watch the news made him acutely aware of the injustices in life. It sickened him to watch innocent children hurt from stray bullets, starvation, and pedophiles. He flipped through the channels and stopped when he saw Allison Rogers. She hated unfairness as much as he. And, like him, she was a crusader.

She was reporting the story of an eighty-two year old man who was swindled by someone who claimed to be in contact with the man's deceased wife. He was left devastated, robbed of his money, and heartbroken.

From the first time he saw the reporter, there was something about her that clicked with him. He felt connected to her, kindred souls. He wanted to, no, HAD to meet her.

It was three in the afternoon when he parked outside the television station. He wanted to catch Allison before she entered the building. By six o'clock, he knew he had missed her. Filled with anticipation, he walked through the lobby doors.

"May I help you?" asked the pleasant, middle-aged woman perched behind the front desk. Before he could respond, "Hello, this is Channel Six, Beth speaking. How may I direct your call?" She turned back to him. "Sorry about that, Sir. Now, may I help you?"

"I'd like to see Allison Rogers."

"Do you have an appointment?" She took three more calls. "I apologize, Sir, but any time Allison is in the studio we are inundated with calls."

"Before you take another one," his fist clenched in his pocket, "I DON'T have an appointment, but I NEED to see her."

Beth pushed her chair back a bit from the counter. "Without a prior arrangement, that would be impossible. But if you'd like to leave a note, I'll see that she gets it."

He relaxed his tense jaw, feigned a smile, and plucked the sheet of paper from her hand but waved away the ballpoint pen. He preferred to use his Mont Blanc.

Disappointed at not meeting Allison, he finished the note and signed it, Your Loyal Fan, H.O.K. He liked the ring of that, H.O.K.

With perfect penmanship, he wrote her name on the outside of the folded paper and boldly underlined 'Personal.'

He approached Beth's desk and found her engaged in conversation again. Without asking, he reached across her desk, took her stapler, and sealed the folded note.

"That'll keep it private." He dropped the note in front of Beth who nodded and continued talking.

He stepped out into the crisp evening air heavy with the scent of night-blooming jasmine. The fragrance soothed his frustration.

"You'll want to see me when you read my note, Allison."

#

"Great job, Allison," Mark Patrick the anchorman called as she left the building carrying an envelope filled with messages Beth had handed her.

The fragrance of jasmine blooming next to the parking lot overawed Allison. She felt heady. "I wonder if Mr. Charles Gabriel enjoyed the show as much as I did." She gloated walking through the lot and paid little attention to the lone sedan parked across the street. The security guard at the T.V. station's parking lot gate waived to her when she reached her car.

Emma wouldn't be home from Chicago til the end of the week so Allison called her on the drive home. They talked until she had replayed the highlights of the show and shared every nuance of the program.

The events of the last hours had Allison too keyed up to sleep. She decided to go through the messages she'd brought home when she discovered she'd left her purse and the envelope Beth had handed her, on the passenger seat. She disarmed the house alarm and ran out to the car.

The front door slammed shut. "Oh crap!" She grabbed her things and ran to the house, relieved to find the door hadn't locked when the wind blew it closed. She bolted the door behind her, set the alarm, and went back to bed.

Allison woke from a dead sleep. A thump. A creak on the stairs. Footsteps in the hall. Someone's here! She dialed 9-1-1.

"Somebody's in my house," she whispered. "Three zero two Belleview Boulevard. Please hurry." She ran and locked the door. The knob turned from the other side.

She screamed to the dispatcher, "Oh God, hurry!" Just then the door rattled.

"I have a gun," she bluffed. "You open the door and I'll shoot." She screamed, "The police are on their way!"

"You're dead, whore!" He kicked the door at the center so hard strips of wood flew across the room.

She fell back. The phone flew from her hand and landed under the bed.

For an instant she thought she recognized the man, but in her panic her thoughts were to flee. She lunged past him. He held her by the hair.

He swung and hit her on the side of her head.

Her nails raked across his face.

Powerful hands clutched her neck.

She gripped his genitals and twisted.

"NO-O-O" he screamed and threw her against the broken door frame. "You fucking, bitch!"

Large splinters ripped her flesh. She scrambled on hands and knees to escape, crawling toward the hallway.

His hands tightened around her neck from behind and lifted her off the floor. "FUCKING WHORE!"

She summoned the last of her strength and clobbered his face with the back of her head. His teeth cut into her scalp.

She dropped to the floor.

Sirens!

CHAPTER THIRTY-NINE

In spite of the fact that repairs had been made, Allison chose to sleep in another bedroom. Even so, she wouldn't feel at peace in her home until the attacker was caught.

She didn't believe she was a victim of a botched home invasion as the police suggested. It was more personal.

#

On Tuesday the doctor gave her a clean bill of health—on Wednesday she had filled her calendar through the next week. She called Steve DeMarcou for an update on her attacker. Before they hung up she had accepted his invitation to lunch.

She offered him her hand but he gave her a tender hug instead and asked how she felt.

"I'd feel better if you told me they caught the guy. After all, how hard is it to find a man with a face full of scratches, a missing front tooth, and walks like he was just gelded?"

Steve winced, then, complimented her on how well she defended herself. "Don't worry, we'll get him."

Allison found the amiable side of him attractive. She wanted to share what she had learned about the pouches and guided the conversation to the colored stones. "Remember when you asked me about them?"

A long pause . . . "Yes."

"I was getting my nails done and a customer seated next to me bragged about a psychic who was telling me about—"

"Allison, I didn't invite you to lunch to talk about psychics."

"You're right. My mistake." *Will I ever learn?*

They finished their meal with polite small talk and discussed the rumors about relocating The Rays to Tampa.

On her way home, Allison felt sad and a little hurt. Their afternoon had started off so well and ended so chilled. "Why does every conversation with Steve end up making me feel like crap? And, why do I keep going back for more?"

CHAPTER FORTY

He stood naked in the living room and stared at the blaring television. "The headless body of a child was found in a plastic bag washed up on the shore near Davis Beach. The body has been identified as that of eight-year-old Kelly Barrett who has been missing for the last two weeks."

"We're in St. Petersburg, outside of the Barrett home," said the reporter. The camera scanned the dilapidated cracker house where the victim lived with her single mother.

"Child Protective Services had been called to the home twice in the last year. Jennifer Barrett, the victim's mother, has not been ruled out as a suspect."

H.O.K's throat tightened as he listened to the mother's ex-boyfriend Ray Castrovic, talking to the reporter. "She was a mean drunk, a party girl; used to wallop on her daughter real good." Ray Castrovic shook his head. "I tried to get her to stop, but she wouldn't. She was so jealous of that child. I couldn't take it no more, so I left."

The station cut away to a clip of Jennifer Barrett on the morning her daughter was discovered missing. She pleaded with the person who took Kelly, to please bring her home. She loved her so very much.

H.O.K. slammed his fist into his opened hand. "Do you know

what should happen to mothers like you? I can't be fooled by those phony tears. I know a rotten mother when I see one."

He called his boss from the car and told Mr. Dakota that he was taking time off. His elderly mother was very ill and he had to care for her. He'd probably be fired when he returned but he didn't give a flying fuck about the job. What he was doing was far more important.

Every day for a week he watched her and every day the evil mother walked to the liquor store and carried home a brown paper bag. The way she dressed in tight jeans and bare midriff disgusted him.

She didn't see him when he drove by. He slipped the picture of Kelly out of his shirt pocket.

"Ten times over, little one," he said. "She'll pay ten times over."

#

The sun had set by the time he pulled between two parked cars to make sure he wasn't being followed.

It was ten thirty when the lights went out in the bungalow. With his bag slung over his shoulder, he walked through the unkempt lawn to the side of the house where an array of trash was piled.

A security bar in the sliding glass door! "Damn," he cursed. The light in the kitchen turned on. He ducked out of the glow and waited.

The woman opened the back door to let out the cat. H.O.K. smelled the rank odor of stale tobacco and alcohol as she stood in the open doorway and lit a cigarette.

His patience wore thin. *I could take her now. No, stick to your plan.*

She flicked the butt into the yard close to where he hid. She shut and locked the door. He moved closer and peered through a gap in the broken blinds.

She stumbled to the cabinet, grabbed a liquor bottle and a glass, switched off the light, and disappeared from down the hall.

He waited in the darkness until he felt it was time. A pat on his shirt pocket assured him the pouch was there. The piss poor lock on the kitchen door made his job easy. He closed it quietly behind him.

The smell of the rancid litter box made him gag.

Once her snores were a steady cadence—*a good sign*—he followed the sounds. The room where he found her was dimly lit by the street lamp that shined through the thin curtains. She lay atop the comforter.

At the edge of the bed, he loomed over her. Filled with contempt, he pressed his hand hard over her mouth and nose. Her eyes flashed opened.

She scratched at his hand—kicked and twisted.

His grip tightened until she lost consciousness then carried her small, limp body into the kitchen and dropped her onto a chair. He taped her hands and feet to the rungs.

On the counter next to him was a greasy dish towel. He picked it up; a cockroach ran out. He stuffed the infested cloth into the unconscious woman's mouth and duct taped it into place.

Next, he took the ammonia capsule from his bag, "You have to be awake for this," and snapped it open under her nose. After she started to rouse, he dropped the used packet into his duffel. Unmoved by the wild look of terror in her eyes, he flashed the steel blade of his hunting knife in front of her before he laid it on the tarp he brought.

In the filth of the room, he tripped over a box of garbage bags lying next to an overstuffed trash basket in front of the sink. He held one up in front of her.

"Are these the same ones you put your little girl into before you dropped her in the bay?"

She shook her head violently. Her body heaved.

He went at her with the hunting knife, twisted his fingers in her hair for leverage, and slashed the razor sharp blade deep into her scrawny neck. Seconds later he snapped her spine, completed the decapitation and discarded the severed head into the garbage bag, dropping it in the duffel. Blood had splattered on the ceiling.

His last act was tossing the pouch of stones onto her blood-soaked lap.

"Karma, sister. Karma."

A car pulled into the driveway. "What the fuck!" Someone approached the front of the house. He threw his tools into his bag and darted for the kitchen door leaving bloody footprints behind. By the time he reached his car, someone screamed.

"Oh, God! Jennifer! Help! Help, somebody!"

The Hand of Karma threw his satchel in and wiped his face of her blood with a sweatshirt lying on the front seat. H.O.K. steered the car away from the scene. Through the opened front door, the figure of a man was crumpled on the floor.

#

The road was all but deserted at that time of the morning. H.O.K. drove east to the causeway, pulled over and pretended to check the tires. Confident the coast was clear he heaved the green trash bag into the bay. Across the bridge, at the opposite end of the causeway, he threw his bloody sneakers one at a time into different areas of the water.

#

It was daylight when he finished cleaning his instruments of Karma. On his way out of the garage, he tossed his work clothes in the dryer and headed to the shower. It took forever to get her blood out of his hair and the smell of that squalor off his skin.

He thought about the deed and the good that would come to him by following the law of retribution. He wanted to bask in the triumph, but first, he needed to write to his mother.

Dear Mom,

Heads up! I've sent you a mother just like you to add to your circle of friends.

As Always, Your Son

CHAPTER FORTY-ONE

Vicky Prince, eyes wet with tears, pulled her over-sized sweater around her as if the weather was below zero, although it was sixty degrees. The winter day in Florida was sunny albeit chilly. She turned on the car's heater as soon as she started the engine and drove around her husband's banged up truck that was parked askew, straddling a small palm tree.

A block before she arrived at Anne Preston's, Vicky pulled off the road and called her. "I'd like to cancel my appointment. I've been thinking about my problems and there are no solutions. No one, not even you can help me. I'll send you a check for your time." She started to hang up.

There was an unmistakable resignation in her voice. "Wait," pleaded Anne. "Please come."

"Why? My life hasn't changed from when I last saw you. My husband is still an alcoholic. My son still has cerebral palsy. My family couldn't care less about me."

"Just come. We'll have a spot of tea and visit." Anne persuaded, "I have the time set aside anyway."

Anne knew what Vicky intended. She was going to take her own life just as Anne once thought of doing to escape a life filled with pain, abuse, and hopelessness.

The awful memories returned.

She relived the day she heard the sickening sing-song voice, "Annie. Uncle Johnny has something for you."

Anne screamed in her head. *You're not going to hurt me anymore. No more dirty pictures, no more touching you, no more poking me!*

"No more," she shouted out loud but the memories wouldn't stop.

"Annie, I know you're down there." He arrived at the top of the stairs, unzipped his pants, and slipped his hand inside. He called to the object of his perverted affection.

"Annie. Annie."

Uncle Johnny strained to see into the darkness at the bottom of the cellar stairs, turned on the light, then hesitated for a second, and took two steps down. His pants slipped below his hips. His face was frozen in fear when he tumbled head first, bouncing and hitting the rest of the steps to the concrete floor. A small pool of blood formed by the side of his head. His neck was bent at an unnatural angle. He was conscious but unable to move. His eyes locked on Annie as she slowly descended the stairs.

Her eyes fixed on his. She stepped over his bent torso. A sliver of wood from the broken banister protruded from his thigh.

Divine Justice—that's what her foster mother called it when someone got punished for breaking house rules.

"I hate you!" she said, through clenched teeth. She grabbed the shovel near the stairs. In one motion, she brandished it with the vehemence of a jungle animal escaped from its torturous master. When she was done, she dropped the shovel next to his cracked skull.

"Poor Uncle Johnny. Did you hurt your head on the shovel?"

Annie clutched the hand of her younger foster sister, Janie, as they watched the hearse slowly pull away with Uncle Johnny's body. She wiped away a single tear.

"Don't be sad, Annie. I'm glad he's dead. He hurt me."

"I'm not sad, Janie."

"Then why are you crying?"

"These are happy tears."

The hearse disappeared down the street. Annie looked at Janie. She knew what he had done to her, too.

#

Dressed in matching navy blue, dotted Swiss dresses, Annie and Janie entered the living room. They liked their new foster home and were happy they were able to stay together. Annie liked school, and so did Janie until the bully, Billy Tate, started to torment her every day. She begged him to stop, but he wouldn't. Now, she'd feel safe going to school.

"Come here, girls," their new foster-mother, Florence, said. She straightened their hats and smiled with satisfaction. They were perfect.

"We need to get going or we'll be late for poor Billy's funeral."

The girls walked to the car, fingers entwined. Janie's eyes filled with tears of gratitude.

"Thank you, Annie."

Billy Tate wouldn't hurt her after school anymore.

#

The outer door opened, jarring Anne from her memories. Vicky had arrived.

Anne sat next to her on the sofa, rather than at her desk. She held Vicky's hand and spoke to her for more than an hour as if she were a dear friend.

". . . And now do you understand how you can turn your life around? How you can have a better future?"

"Anne, do you really think I can do it? After all, I have so many problems."

"Of course you can. Vicky, no one's family is perfect, but I do have to admit mine was pretty close. Try to make the best of whatever your circumstances may be."

"Anne, how can I thank you for caring so much?"

"I ask you for only two things. First, keep your promise to see a psychiatrist." Anne handed Vicky a patchouli scented pouch containing stones. "And second, you must meditate every day as I instructed you and hold those close to your heart when you do. They'll help you on your journey."

CHAPTER FORTY-TWO

SERIAL KILLER OR VIGILANTE. No further details have turned up since the discovery of the decapitated body of Jennifer Barrett, mother of slain eight-year-old Kelly Barrett whose body was found in Tampa Bay two weeks ago. It is believed that Jennifer Barrett may be the victim of a serial killer who has been dubbed the 'Stone Killer' by the media because of stones found at the murder sites of other victims.

Police have reason to believe that there may be a link between the murder of Jennifer Barrett who was decapitated like her daughter and the death of Jesse Charles Lee last month in the rural town of Crestview, Florida.

His body was found naked and beaten to death in a heavily wooded area off Highway 90 close to his home. Similar evidence was found near the body. Lee, 28, was out on $40,000 bond. He had been accused of scalding the two-year-old son of his girlfriend while she was at work.

The killer's trademark is the only connection

found between any of the eight known victims of the Stone Killer.

A marked increase in gun sales has been reported statewide.

At today's press conference Sheriff Ken Brown stressed there is no difference between someone who is a vigilante or a serial killer.

"Citizens cannot take the law into their own hands. You can't be judge, jury, and executioner," he said. "We'll get you."

A special task force, led by Sgt. Geoff Vernon of the Pinellas County Sheriff's Office, is working with other Florida agencies to piece together this puzzle. There is a reward of $75,000 for information leading to the arrest and conviction of this person or persons. If you have any information, call Crime Stoppers or 911. You can remain anonymous.

How ironic that Allison's help with 'no strings attached' had been rejected by the police. But they're offering a $75,000 reward to Mr. or Mrs. Anonymous.

Emma called from downstairs that dinner was ready. Allison wadded the newspaper and tossed it in 'File 13.' She had a hectic week coming up but would drive to Crestview as soon as her schedule cleared.

CHAPTER FORTY-THREE

Her cell phone dropped to the ground as Allison reached the car. She picked up several pieces and dropped them into her bag. As much as she wanted to tell her sister about the psychic reading she had at the little bookstore, she'd have to wait until she got home. Funny, she thought, the reader had mentioned she would have communication problems. She didn't expect it to happen so soon.

They sat by the pool while Allison recapped her afternoon. "Poor thing was as skinny as a rail; wore coke bottle glasses and way too many gold chains; had a ring on every finger; and his shirt was unbuttoned so far I could see he had a carpet on his chest. God! That was a visual I didn't need. But, this part I couldn't make up if I tried. His name is Tommy Gunn!"

Allison continued, "I have to admit I didn't expect him to be so thorough and accurate. He knew that my California office had been ransacked, that someone I loved was murdered, and that the person I live with, loves me very much. When he finished the reading, he complimented me on my investigations! He hoped I'd give him a favorable review."

"He was right on the money with everything. Just goes to show you can't judge a book by its cover."

Screech! They turned in unison to see a bald eagle fly away from the dock with a fish in its talons. They watched in silence until the eagle soared out of sight.

"How breathtaking." Emma turned to her sister. "So where were we?"

"After the reading he handed me a couple of polished stones. Said they were for good luck. There I was holding them, wondering how to keep them from disappearing into the black hole inside my purse when he handed me a little chamois sack. Of all things, it reeked of rose oil. You know how I hate the smell of roses."

She didn't dare tell Emma she had a hunch about the leather bag and how she got the supplier's name from Tommy Gunn and planned to meet with her. If her sister knew, she'd blow a gasket! But, she would tell Steve.

"I was just going to call you," Steve said. "We arrested Armando Tiberi—Madame Marie's son. He's the one who attacked you."

Weak in the knees, Allison sat down on the ottoman by the window. "Madame Marie's son? How'd he know where I live?"

"Channel Six ran the promos about your live report. He knew where you were going to be. He only had to watch, wait, and follow you home."

"That dirt bag! Now what's going to happen?"

"We've got him locked up. I promise, he's going nowhere but jail."

"But for how long?"

"For as long as the law allows."

Whatever it was going to be, wouldn't be satisfactory for her.

Steve said, "Armando also confessed he almost got you at the mall. He was really pissed when you tried to run him over."

"Too bad I didn't!"

"You're something else, Allison. I wouldn't want to cross you. I guess I won't need to volunteer to be your body guard!"

If only you would. She didn't want to push Steve away again. She would wait to tell him about the pouch and Tommy Gunn.

He interrupted her thoughts. "Hey, you called me."

"It's okay. You've answered my question."

CHAPTER FORTY-FOUR

The dream came again. Footsteps, a high window, no way out! Instead of the attacker this time, it was Steve who appeared in the doorway and carried her to the bed. Allison awakened from her dream and felt like a giddy school girl.

She'd already showered and dressed before the alarm clock went off. Ready for an early start, she drove off to the small town of Ozona to meet the seamstress.

Suede vests, fanny packs, draw string bags, and other leather goods covered the walls and tables. "Mrs. Carpenter, Tommy Gunn said you're the only one his store buys their leather bags from because your work is always perfect."

"Ain't he sweet, now? But, you know anybody can make a nice pouch. What makes my product unique is that each order gets scented with a different essential oil. And, no two vendors get the same one."

"Wonderful. I'm in the market for small purses, about the size of a deck of cards. The scent should be something earthy—patchouli would be perfect. Do you have that?"

"I do, but patchouli is already taken. As I said, I never duplicate."

Allison pried and asked if the customer might trade with her.

Mrs. Carpenter was adamant that Ms. Preston would never change. It was her signature scent.

"But, I do have a spicy musk I'm sure you'll really like."

Allison took the sample and told the woman she'd think about it and be in touch.

#

The head of the Stone Killer task force, Sergeant Geoff Vernon, greeted Allison Rogers. He said he had seen her on television and regretted he had no more than five minutes to spare but politely asked what he could do for her.

Allison placed the pouch on his desk. She told him that they're given out by several local psychics. One in particular, Anne Preston, used them scented with patchouli which was the same fragrance Allison had psychically detected at the Tropicana Field crime scene.

He sat in silence and scratched his head as if he was trying to decide what to say next.

"Sergeant, I'd like to give you the name and address of the woman who makes these," and handed him a slip of paper.

"Mrs. Rogers, this is a murder investigation. You need to stick to checking out psychics. For your own safety and for the integrity of this case, please let us handle it." He stood. "If you'll excuse me now . . ."

After she left, he read the note Allison gave him then made a call.

"Jerry, I need you to follow up on some—thing and some—one. Come in to my office when you get a second."

CHAPTER FORTY-FIVE

"He is guilty and he's going to get away with murder!" She hung up abruptly.

The Hand of Karma knew what he must do.

Community activist, Freddy Harlan, confessed to killing his step-daughter after hours of interrogation. "I drowned her like a sack of kittens cause she kept making false accusations against me."

\#

A couple of blocks away from the office of attorney Donna Smythe, H.O.K. parked his car. He had to fight through a crowd of protesters demonstrating in front of the Church of Scientology headquarters in order to reach his destination. A throng of reporters, who waited on the steps of the Clearwater Courthouse for Freddy Harlan to appear after his hearing, pushed H.O.K. aside, forcing him to settle for a place closer to the sidewalk as onlookers encroached on his space.

The courthouse doors opened and Freddy Harlan emerged flashing a wide grin. Freddy was a free man! His attorney, Donna Smythe, flanked him.

The Hand of Karma made eye contact with him. Freddy

nodded and turned away.

Reporters shouted questions at Smythe. "Don't you feel any remorse for getting Harlan set free?"

"As Mr. Harlan's attorney, it is my job to present the best possible defense."

Another reporter asked, "How can you represent someone who has confessed to drowning a child?"

"I am obligated to give the best defense within the guidelines of the law. That should force prosecutors to do a better job!" She held up her hand. "Please, please," she said, "no more questions. I'll make one statement at this time. Judge Potter has ruled that the coerced statements made by Mr. Harlan cannot be used against him. The police ignored his repeated requests to have an attorney present, thereby disregarding his constitutional rights. Furthermore, there is not, and never was, any evidence connecting Mr. Harlan to the unfortunate death of his step-daughter, Ashley Bauer."

H.O.K. said to no one in particular, "She's as guilty as he is. She knows what he did." He yelled at the liars as they pushed past the reporters. "Constitutional rights my ass! Doesn't Ashley have rights, too?"

There's no escape from Karma.

The converted Spanish-style house that boasted Smythe and Smythe, P.A., Attorneys at Law, was in the older section of Clearwater, an area not yet bought up by the Church of Scientology. A lone television truck sat in the lot farther down the street. Hunkered down behind the wheel of the Toyota, H.O.K. watched as Harlan and Smythe hurried into the law office.

What a stroke of luck. Two for one! He checked his knapsack which lay on the seat next to him. Plenty of supplies for a two-fer. This will be the last office visit Harlan will have with his attorney.

The side door of the office building opened up to the parking lot. A silver-haired woman left the building. She climbed into her Mini Cooper and drove off.

He checked his rearview mirror. The demonstrators were dispersing from the front of the courthouse. It was almost five o'clock. He slipped on his baseball cap and work gloves, checked the street again, took his supplies, and left the car.

The front door of the law office was unlocked. *A good sign.* Inside the vestibule, he turned the deadbolt, secured the wooden door, and entered the deep green and burgundy reception area. They were talking in another room and it sounded like they were getting ready to leave. He had to act fast!

Harlan walked out first with Smythe following close behind him. He bashed Harlan in the face with the tire iron and watched as the man fell backward through the doorway, smack into the bewildered woman. She fell to the floor.

A quick and hard blow from the tire iron landed against her head.

Harlan choked on the blood from his shattered nose and mouth. The next blow came to the side of his head cracking his skull like an egg.

The woman, flat on her back, gurgled.

H.O.K. reached into his bag to retrieve the duct tape, but changed his mind. There'd be no need. Smythe convulsed. "Here's your Constitutional rights, counselor. It's called Karma." With a fierce blow from the tire iron, he crushed her throat.

He withdrew jogging shorts and a tee shirt from a plastic bag which he had organized in anticipation of this event. With the calm of a snake shedding its skin, he peeled off his bloody clothes, shoved them into the plastic bag then stuffed it and the tire iron into the knapsack. Donned in his change of clothes, he would blend in with everyone else on the street.

He tossed the bag of stones near the bodies and left by the back door.

#

The door of the news van swung open and Treena Montgomery, dressed in a business suit, climbed out. She smoothed her hair, and straightened her blouse.

"Come on, Jimmy. If we hurry, we might catch them leaving the building. And, if the TV gods are with us, we'll get this in for the early news. Be sure to get a good shot of the sign for my intro."

They hurried across the street and were on their way to the front door of the law office; the camera balanced on Jimmy's shoulder.

The news woman tried the door but it was locked. She knocked several times but got no answer and then motioned for Jimmy to 'start rolling.'

"Mrs. Smythe, this is Treena Montgomery from Channel Eight. We know you're in there. We'd like to give you the opportunity to share your side of the story on Mr. Harlan's case."

Treena's cajoling went unanswered. She told Jimmy to turn off the camera. "Go around back in case they try to sneak out that way," she whispered.

In a minute, Jimmy returned. "Hey, Treena, the back door is wide open. Somethin' ain't right."

#

He was sure no one saw him leave. H.O.K. had planned to approach his car from a different direction by circling around the block first. He turned right as he exited the building, then, vaulted over a low, wooden fence and started to walk at a nonchalant pace. He came upon a discarded protest sign lying on the ground.

"Another good sign—in every sense of the word," he bent down to pick it up. He carried the sign another couple of blocks before turning right again.

Sirens wailed. They came closer.

"Ah shit!"

He quickened his pace and rounded the corner; the safety of his car was seconds away. Alarmed, he watched a Clearwater cop approach the Toyota. Before he could react, the officer called to him.

"Is this your vehicle, sir?"

He stopped dead in his tracks. Unable to speak, he nodded. The officer shook his head at the sign he held.

"Protest is over," the cop barked. "It's one hour parking here. Move this vehicle before I give you a ticket."

An ambulance stopped in front of the law office. H.O.K.'s self-control hid his panic. The carrion wasn't supposed to be found until he was long gone.

"I said, get this vehicle out of here!" the cop yelled.

"Yes sir," he answered opening the car door. "No problem."

He tossed his backpack and sign onto the seat. A drop of blood on his sneaker caught his eye.

Some trained observer! Stupid cop.

What a rush!

CHAPTER FORTY-SIX

He didn't feel in the clear until he reached the security of his garage. When he stepped out of the car, he noticed a piece of broken tooth stuck to his shoelace. If it hadn't been for the fading daylight, the cop would have seen it for sure. He reached in the glove box for a tissue, wrapped the fragment, and tossed it in the trash.

He knew she'd value his initiative to make the lawyer pay as well. Eager to boast of his accomplishments, he called. Voicemail. Disappointed, he left his message. "Turn on the news and find your gift from me."

He imagined her smile when she learned of the 'bonus' of his mission and knew she'd feel their connection deepen each time he followed her orders because he could feel their union strengthen too. There was one last thing to take care of before he retired for the night.

He opened his journal.

> *Dear Mom and Dad,*
> *Your lucky day! I've sent you two for the price of one. Shouldn't I get brownie points because one's a lawyer?*
>
> *Your Thrifty Son*

He lay down in bed, arms wrapped around a pillow, holding it as if it were she. In his sleep she came to him, kissing him softly, praising him. Her scent was feminine. His dreams were sweet and sexual.

Early in the morning, he woke when she called. "Hello?"

"Saw the news. Good job."

Click.

He sat on the side of his bed and thought of the planning and effort he'd put into his mission, to say nothing of the risk he'd taken. "Good job? That's it? What the fuck? What about, I'm proud of you, partner; or, we make a great team?"

As the day wore on, his unrealized expectations of her praise dragged him to the edge of that dark hole. He was about to succumb to the blackness. Throughout the day, he walked from room to room, holding the pouch and muttering to himself.

The amulets weren't working. They no longer protected him from his demons of despair.

He knew what he had to do to alleviate the torment. The medicine cabinet held his relief. He removed the small box of individually wrapped, single-edged razor blades he kept just for an emergency like this.

He sat on the edge of the tub. A clean wash cloth was unfolded and placed on his lap. His arm rested on his knee. Between his thumb and forefinger he held the shiny new blade and pressed firmly into his forearm, using the old scar as a guide. He gritted his teeth.

Blood ran onto the cloth. Pain. Then relief. He wrapped the wound with gauze then covered it with an Ace bandage.

In spite of his throbbing arm, the ominous dark cloud began to lift. Only a fellow cutter could understand the dichotomy of the process. The emotional pain was released.

CHAPTER FORTY-SEVEN

Los Angeles County, California

"Totah!" Massaro barked as he barged into the room.

She spun around, dropped the file, papers scattered on the floor. "Jesus fucking Christ, Massaro! You scared the shit out of me. Why don't you knock or make some noise when you come in to a room." Her agitation was clear as she picked up the papers.

"Does your mother know about your foul mouth?" Massaro asked.

"Yeah, I've been blowing bubbles out of my ass since I was thirteen. To this day, you can find a cake of soap in my mother's purse!"

"You're a piece of work, Totah," he shook his head.

She placed the file folder on a small table. "Massaro, let me ask you a question. Is there a reason you're so unwilling to see that the wife had motive, means, and opportunity? I know her financial records came back clean, but that doesn't convince me."

"Let me ask you, Totah. Is there a reason you're so biased against her?"

"Yeah. We know Carlos Dominguez pulled the trigger, but I feel it in my bones . . . she was the mastermind. You saw how arrogant she was when you questioned her. Her rich-bitch attitude of

'I know everything. I see everything and you're just a lowly cop!'

"A little insecure? Her turban bigger than yours?"

"She can afford a closet full of turbans on what she'll get from offing her husband, and no I'm not insecure. I love being an underpaid civil servant. " Totah bowed, then said, "Tell you what, Massaro. If I'm wrong, I'll buy you a steak dinner."

"And if you're right," he said, "I'll take you. Deal?"

"Deal."

CHAPTER FORTY-EIGHT

Pinellas County, Florida

"What's this?" Allison found the manila envelope filled with written notes and messages she'd brought from the T.V. station the night she was attacked in her home.

She read them all. Most were Thank you's, words of encouragement, and a couple of callers who took a personal affront to her criticism of psychics. She read one particular message supporting Mr. Gabriel saying she should show more respect. This person accused her of being jealous of his celebrity status.

At the bottom of the pile was a folded paper, stapled, her name written with a fountain pen in distinctive blue ink. For a split second, an image of three colored stones appeared in her mind's eye when she opened it.

Filled with unease she read:

> *Mrs. Rogers,*
> *I greatly admire your work to rid society of undesirables who harm the vulnerable. We have much in common. We must meet soon to discuss our mutual interests.*
>
> *Warmest Regards, H.O.K.*

"Channel Six, this is Beth speaking. How may I help you?"

"Beth, its Allison Rogers. I need ask you some questions. Do you have a minute for me?"

"Sure, what can I do for you?"

"The night I was attacked, a note was left for me. Do you remember?"

"You poor dear! I hope they put that man away for a long time. How're you feeling?"

"I'm fine. It's thoughtful of you to ask, but Beth, I—"

"Did I forget something?"

"No, Beth. Do you remember someone leaving a note for me? A man?"

"That was such a busy night. It always is when you're here."

It was a challenge for Allison to keep the receptionist focused. "Beth, I found a stapled note—"

"Wait a minute, a stapled note . . . let me think . . . yes, there was a man who came in to see you. He didn't have an appointment though. He was a little inpatient."

"Did he leave his name? Can you describe him?" It seemed an eternity had passed while Beth muttered quietly to herself, trying to recall him in detail.

"Does this have something to do with what happened to you?"

"No, Beth! I just need to find out who he is."

"He didn't leave his name and I didn't get a good look at his face. He wore a baseball cap real low, almost covered his eyes. Does that help?"

"Can you recall anything else?"

"I remember he wore a distinctive six-pointed star. I saw it when he reached across my desk to pick up the stapler. I think it was gold. It must have been expensive."

When Beth had finished, Allison thanked her and asked the woman to get in touch with her if he stopped by again.

The man wanted to connect with her. She wondered if she should go to the police. What could she tell them, anyway? A fan left her a nicely written note, and by the way, no one knows what he looks like. Her train of thought was interrupted when someone came to the door.

It was T.D., the station's intern who delivered more flowers that were sent to her at the station.

A dish garden with crystals sprinkled over the moss was from Thomas Gunn. Next, was a small vase of flowers from Beth. The last was a large floral basket.

Elegant handwriting on the card! No florist's identification. The same shade of blue ink! Chills ran up her spine.

> *To An Awesome Lady,*
> *I detest what's happened to you. Recover quickly.*
> *Your Loyal Friend, H.O.K.*

Seated at her desk, she picked up a pencil and listed what she knew about H.O.K.:

- We're 'kindred souls' – I do good exposing con artists – Possible
- Star of David, could be Jewish, Kabala students wear them
- Kabala-Old Testament-Eye for an Eye, Karma
- She remembered 'hearing' "Karma Brother, Karma" at Tropicana Field – connected?
- He knows me!!

Next she listed what she knew about the Stone Killer:

- Flies under radar, ahead of police
- Chooses victims - From where? Public records? Follows trials? The news?

- Patchouli scented pouch with stones. Linked to Anne Preston. Ceremonial? Releasing demons? Do you frequent psychics?
- Dark car
- Fastidious – no prints – no DNA – no witnesses

She paced her room. A nagging thought haunted her. Do you know each other? Or, are you the Stone Killer, H.O.K.?

#

He could hardly believe his good fortune when he took the basket of flowers to the station for Allison and was told by the young girl at the desk that flowers and mail were being delivered to Allison later that day.

Parked under an oak tree from an unobstructed vantage point, he watched until a freckle-faced kid loaded flowers into a van. H.O.K. followed.

#

A muscle spasm in her neck was a reminder of the attack by Armando, Madame Marie's son. She took a break, swallowed a couple aspirin, and lay down. What does H.O.K. mean? Your name? An organization? An acronym? "What are you trying to tell me, H.O.K.?" She dosed off and the dream began:

> *A long stretch of road. A Route 90 sign. A cross marker next to the side of the road. Dense trees. Heavy rain. A body. A dark figure wearing a star on a chain.*

CHAPTER FORTY-NINE

The ride to Crestview took longer than the six hours she had expected. Tired and hungry, Allison pulled into the truck stop on Route 90 near where the body of Jesse Charles Lee had been found. She chatted with people she figured were regulars who were more than willing to discuss the shocking discovery of his body and give her directions to where he was found. She finished her meal and set off to find the place before the forecasted rain.

It was a little ways down the road from what they told her. "You'll come up to a flower-covered cross on the right side."

A tractor trailer hauling pine logs whizzed past her and blasted his air horn as she slowed to pull over. The marker was positioned against a tree alongside the road. Allison stepped gingerly around the fire ant mounds on her way to the cross. *A roaring engine; squealing brakes; metal against metal!* She read the date inscribed on the cross. Two years ago. This was an accident. She was in the wrong place.

OUCH! Something stung her foot. Allison bolted to her car, pulled the stinger out of her toe and emptied her water bottle over it.

Two semi's barreled by before she could pull onto the road. A little farther down the highway, another cross. Parked on the side of the road, she found what she was looking for—the name Jesse Lee was clearly marked on it. She was revolted at the thought of someone scalding a little child. Allison turned away from the cross and exchanged her sandals for socks and sneakers she took from her gym bag in the trunk and chastised herself for not wearing them earlier.

The area beyond the asphalt smelled like it had been freshly mowed. Guided by her instincts, she tromped into the dense woods which were difficult to navigate.

The trees reminded her of the fort she made as a child in the back yard with blankets over the lawn chairs. Under the canopy of pines, what little sunlight had shone through was now obliterated by ominous black clouds.

She wrapped her arms closer to her chest to ward off the chill, trudged deeper into the woods, and crossed a muddy gully. It was there that she picked up the force of the brutal attack on Jesse Lee. The God-awful sounds of him being bludgeoned to death made her stomach turn.

Allison stood motionless for a moment, then images! A black car; a man in dark clothes; a baseball cap. He throws a pouch on the body. The star. Patchouli.

"Karma, brother. Karma."

She spun around in the direction of the voice. No one. Nothing but pines, underbrush, and trash.

A crack of thunder announced the deluge of rain. On the dash to her vehicle, something caught her ankle and sent her crashing down on her knees. She screamed, wrenched her leg free and ran, dragging a piece of tattered crime scene tape that got tangled around her shoe!

By the time she reached the shelter of her car, she was soaked, muddy, and felt foolish.

Too tired to make the long drive home, Allison took a room at the Sleepy Time Motel. She'd leave early in the morning and be home before noon.

Soothed after a hot shower, she left a message for Emma on the answering machine that she would stay the night in Crestview and was thrilled that she wouldn't have to argue her decision, until tomorrow, as to what she was doing in north Florida. Angry with herself that she'd forgotten the car charger for her cell, she turned it off to save the battery.

"Housekeeping," a voice echoed from the corridor outside.

Allison looked at the clock. "It can't be ten a.m. already!"

After a meager attempt to get the mud off the knees of her jeans, she dressed and ate a quick breakfast at the little café attached to the motel, then started for home. No sooner had she turned on her cell, it rang.

"What the hell are you doing in Crestview?"

"Good morning, Emma."

"Don't 'good morning' me!"

"Emma, I'll tell you all about it when I get home. Forgot my charger. Low battery. Love ya. Bye."

The phone rang before she could put it away. Anticipating an argument with her sister, she was hesitant to answer.

"Yes?"

"Allison, this is Anne Preston. You and I got off on the wrong foot. I must admit, I too, was at fault. I'm mortified by my outburst the other day. I'd like to apologize properly. May I take you to lunch Friday?"

"Yes! Can we meet at twelve, E & E in Belleair?"

"That would be delightful. There's so much I want to—"

The phone died.

CHAPTER FIFTY

It was a beautiful sunny day when Allison arrived to find Anne seated at a table on the patio of the restaurant. A hummingbird hovered over a hanging flower basket next to them.

They sipped their Cosmopolitans and discussed the ambiance of the garden patio while they waited for their lunch. Anne commented, "I'm so fond of the name, 'Allison.' That was my darling mother's name."

"That's a nice coincidence," Allison stated.

"Yes it is. But then, life is full of coincidences isn't it?" Anne waited until the waiter walked away before she spoke again. "As you know, the reporter you sent caught me off guard. I do hope you'll forgive my rudeness when I called you."

Allison nodded. "And I am sorry I over-stepped my bounds."

"Perhaps if I simplify it for you, Allison, you'll understand. You see, my father was old-fashioned. He was loving and generous, but strict about protecting our privacy in business and personal matters. He taught us to never let anyone get too close. He was adamant! To this day I remember his words, 'Trust no one but family.'"

Allison volunteered, "My father was an engineer. What kind of business was your father in, may I ask?"

"The market. But that's not important. I hoped you and I could make a fresh start today." Anne smiled politely. "I wanted to tell you, I feel dreadful about your recent accident."

"I think, Anne, you of all people would know it was no accident."

"You're right, of course!" Anne smoothed the napkin on her lap. Her voice quieted. "I did try to warn you."

"I haven't forgotten your warning. Now, allow me to return the favor. I've sensed something I would like to share with you. It's about one of your clients."

"Please," Anne tensed. "I doubt there's anything you can tell me that I don't already know."

"Excuse me?" Allison's eyebrow arched.

"Don't be offended. I simply know what you're going to say."

"I wouldn't be too sure."

"Allison, there's no need to be so defensive. I only meant—"

"Ladies, was everything okay? Would you like to have dessert?"

"No. Thank you. We're finished." Anne handed the waiter fifty dollars. "This should cover everything. Allison, it's been enjoyable, but I must run." She rose to leave, "I almost forgot. I brought you a little something." She reached into her purse, "You may find these helpful," and placed a small gift bag on the table. "Cheerio," she said, and walked away.

Allison shook her head at the ridiculous affectation, 'Cheerio,' and turned her attention to the gift bag. She reached inside.

"Oh!"

#

"Sergeant Vernon, I thought you might be interested in this." Allison handed him the pouch and stones that Anne Preston had given her at lunch and watched him examine it.

"Mrs. Rogers, I don't mean to be rude, but didn't I make myself clear the last time you gave me a pouch? This is a police matter!"

"Sergeant, will you at least let me tell you what I've discovered?"

"Discovered, how?"

166

"I'll get to that, but first let me tell you this . . ." She went on to explain about going to the crime scenes and what she saw about the killer. She reminded him about Mrs. Carpenter, the lady who made the pouches, and the patchouli scented connection to Anne Preston and that Anne's the only one that scents the bags with patchouli.

"He may be someone she reads for! He's going to kill again, and soon. You've got to do something!"

"Okay, Mrs. Rogers." He crossed his arms and exhaled. "Can you be more specific about the killer?"

She despised his patronizing tone, but ignored it and continued. "He's white, has an average build, wears a baseball cap, and I think he may be Jewish. And—"

"What makes you think he's Jewish?"

"He wears a Star of David."

"Mrs. Rogers, d'ya ever turn on MTV? Half the rock stars and rappers wear 'em."

"Sergeant," her frustration mounted. "He drives an older model, black car—"

"What's the plate number?"

"I never saw the license plate!" She steadied her gaze. "But, I believe his initials are H.O.K.!"

"Okay, Mrs. Rogers. I'll bite." He opened a pack of cigarettes. "What makes you think his initials are H.O.K.? Is that a psychic vision?"

"Yes . . . no, I mean, I received a note, then a card with flowers. Both cards were signed by someone using the initials H.O.K."

"Did he confess?"

"No, but—"

"Were the notes threatening?"

"No. I just—"

"Did he say anything in them that ties him to the murders?" He placed the unlit cigarette in the corner of his mouth.

"I psychometrized the notes and made a list of things for you to evaluate." She placed the list in front of him. "Dammit, Sergeant!

His energy is terrifying!"

"Mrs. Rogers, I can't tell my deputies to be on the lookout for a non-descript white man, wearing jewelry and a baseball cap, driving a dark car, who has terrifying energy."

"He's going to kill again," her voice cracked in frustration, "and soon. And, something else—at every location I explore, I hear the words, 'Karma, brother. Karma.'"

"Karma? You mean like an eye for an eye."

She saw the pointlessness of her efforts and rose to leave. "Thank you, sergeant, for your time."

"And, Mrs. Rogers . . . I don't want to tell you again. Stay away from the investigation."

Allison slammed the door as she left.

Sergeant Vernon held the pouch and said to himself, "Yes, Mrs. Rogers, we are already aware of Anne Preston."

Shortly after Allison left Sergeant Vernon's office Detective Sean O'Keefe, a member of the task force, showed up.

"Hey, Sarge, I got this call from a reporter. He lives in St. Pete now—moved here four years ago. Gave me a story about a serial killer in Oregon. This guy covered it.

"I made some calls, turns out the subject is a thirty-eight-year-old insurance adjuster. He was linked to four torture homicides similar to our Stone Killer. But their guy left a bag of dried stuff at the scenes. Crap like sage, lavender, and a feather. Get this, his vics were all sex offenders who walked."

Vernon sat up. "Could it be the same guy? You think we got a vigilante?"

"That's what I was thinking. I'll keep you posted."

An hour later, O'Keefe returned holding a fax.

"Can you believe this shit? The prick from Oregon caught the big one in custody. Guess we got another dead-end."

CHAPTER FIFTY-ONE

The beautiful Victorian house that stood on a large lot facing Lake Magdeline in Tampa, appeared unchanged since it was built. It was the home of Catherine Donaldson. Allison noted that in the small office attached to Catherine's home, there were no holy pictures or statues; no crystal ball, not even a candle. The only adornments were plant stands filled with flowers.

She didn't expect to see a psychic in her late seventies. When she called as 'Martha Baker' to make arrangements for the meeting, the voice of the seer was youthful.

Catherine apologized for the ten minute wait and ran her hand over her snow white hair to smooth loose ends back into her chignon.

"I've never seen so many beautiful African Violets in one place," Allison complimented. "You must have a green thumb."

"Oh, it's not my green thumb. It's all of the good vibrations I'm surrounded with in this room, from people like you!" Catherine said, "If you've brought a cassette player with you, you're welcome to record our visit." She took out a pack of old playing cards that had been laminated to preserve them and reassured 'Martha' that she used them only as a crutch, so to speak.

"They have no influence on their own, but when I have you shuffle and hold them, your essence is infused into the cards and I'm able to go into greater detail about what I see for you."

The reader recounted in great detail Allison's childhood and background. She was told to expect a large amount of money, but it would be coming from a place of happiness and pain.

"A strong and gentle woman vacillates between admiration for you and professional jealousy. Be careful where you place your trust.

"Someone believes you are guilty of a terrible crime."

Her words stung. Allison knew she was still a person of interest in Kent's murder, but to hear those words spoken, stunned her.

"And, if you meditate, you will see the face of the true criminal who killed your husband."

Allison interrupted, "I've tried!"

"Perhaps you are trying too hard. Just relax and let it rise to your consciousness. It will come to you." Catherine continued. "Your path keeps crossing with a man who appears harmless, but is not. His deeds are horrendous and he has lost control of his mind. Consider him like a poppy which starts out as a beautiful flower that can be developed into a medicinal opiate, or manipulated into something destructive and deadly. Beware! You are being drawn into his madness!"

Catherine reached across the small table and gathered up the cards. "I feel your displeasure that I can't tell you who he is." Apology showed in her clear blue eyes.

"I understand that psychics don't know everything," Allison said, "but, thank you for what you've given me."

"Before you leave, it wasn't necessary to wear a disguise 'Martha.' You couldn't conceal who you are to me!"

Pages of emails from victims of psychic scams throughout the state waited for Allison's replies. In spite of all the work that had stacked up and a deadline hanging over her, she needed to unwind before she tackled the chore.

She filled the Jacuzzi, lit candles, sprinkled lavender bath salts into the water, and stepped into the tub. Perfect. The bubbling water came up to her chest. She laid her head back, closed her eyes, and felt tranquil as the fragrance and sound of the water calmed her.

Memories of California drifted through her mind. Her first date with Kent, the honeymoon, Kent carrying her over the threshold . . . *Carlos Dominguez!*

"Oh my, God!" She climbed out of the tub, wrapped herself in a towel, her feet slippery on the wet marble tiles, and ran to her room. The phone rang as she reached for it.

"Mrs. Rogers, this is Detective Massaro. I've got some news. We found out who murdered your husband. The man was Carlos Dominguez. His wife Christina came to see you on several occasions."

"Yes, I know who she is. I was just—"

He talked right through her and continued giving her the update on Carlos Dominguez and how they discovered he'd killed Kent.

It was guilt she felt, not relief. Her mind was filled with 'if onlys' and 'coulda, shoulda, woulda's.' She knew in some convoluted way she was responsible for Kent's death. So many people affected. What a lousy conclusion for Kent's life; a life that had so much promise.

CHAPTER FIFTY-TWO

Determined to leave regrets behind, Allison tried to maintain a positive outlook. One resolution was to complete her manuscript before summer but more research was needed. In spite of admonishments from her sister to slow down, she pushed herself to the point of near exhaustion.

#

Louise Livingston, the 'seer who could break curses,' did little more than cleanse Allison's wallet of sixty dollars. She arrived home tired and slipped off her shoes. The message light blinked on the answering machine.

"Hey, Allison. It's a voice from the past—Steve DeMarcou. I tried to reach you on your cell. I'll call you later."

Hmmm.

As the messages played, she checked her cell. She'd forgotten to turn it back on after her meeting with Louise Livingston.

The next message was from Emma. "Allison, I'll be late. Take out the steaks."

Then: "Allison. It's Steve again. I was wondering if you like Italian food. There's this great restaurant in Tampa. Let me know if you'd like to go sometime."

That sounded like a date. She remembered their lunch at R.G.'s and considered declining his offer.

"Oh hell!" She had to eat. Besides, she really did want to see him.

She waited until the next morning to call Steve and accepted his invitation to dinner.

CHAPTER FIFTY-THREE

Allison charged through the front door.

"Emma, where are you?"

"Do you have to enter the house like a tornado?"

"Save the speech. Wait til I tell you what I did. I went to Tampa where that guy's body was found under the overpass—"

"Allison, are you trying to get yourself killed or tempting me to Baker Act you?"

"Wait. There's going to be another Stone Killing before next month."

Emma scowled and placed the cup of tea on the counter with a purposeful *Clink*.

"Who?" Allison. "How? Where?"

"What's wrong with you, Emma? You're supposed to be on my side."

"I am, but I don't want to see you go through what I did when I was naïve like you."

"But, what if I can save someone?"

"Sometimes you can't, Allison. Do you remember when I retired?"

"Yeah—when you married Harry."

"No. It was after the police asked me about the Boston Strangler. Another psychic, Peter Hurkos, had worked on the investigation. Like Hurkos, I said De Salvo wasn't the Boston Strangler, it was his cell mate. Most in law enforcement thought De Salvo was guilty. He was a sick-o criminal, and was convicted, but, he wasn't the Strangler."

"What's your point, Emma?"

"Cops from Boston to Florida made jokes about me."

"Didn't they do the same to Hurkos?"

"Of course. But he must have had thicker skin. For God's sake Allison, the newspapers made me out to be a board certified nut. The tabloids put the story in next to an alien abduction report about a woman who had a big-eyed, no-ears baby.

Although he never mentioned it, I'm sure Harry was uncomfortable at work. Now, am I getting through to you?"

"But you were proven right!" Allison stressed.

"Sure. It took ten years. The damage was already done."

"What do you suggest I do?"

"I suggest you slow down. You've spread yourself too thin. You're working on your book, you've got the television show, and now you're giving lectures. For crying out loud, Allison, you've become obsessed with the Stone Killer murders."

Allison shook her head, "Thanks for the advice, Sis," and walked away.

"Before I forget," Emma called after her. "A certified letter came for you today. It's on the hall table."

She held the envelope, confused as to why Kent's attorney, Ted Hawkins, would be sending her a letter. She tore it open. "Oh . . . my . . . God!"

"What? What?" Emma rushed to her.

"I can't believe it." Allison took a couple of deep breaths. "It says because we never divorced, and Kent specified it in his Will, I'm the sole beneficiary of Kent's estate! And here's a copy of the Will. There's the lawyer's number for me to call." Her hand shook as she dialed the phone.

After the call, an astounded Allison turned to Emma, "He left it all to me! The attorney said he insisted on it, even though we were in the middle of a divorce." In disbelief, she continued, "He updated his Will right before he was murdered."

Emma pursed her lips. "Sounds to me like Kent felt guilty. No wonder the police suspected you!"

CHAPTER FIFTY-FOUR

The dream was so real, that when Allison woke, she felt Kent's presence in the room. In the dream, he repeated, 'It wasn't what it looked like,' and, 'I'm sorry I hurt you.' Sadness and an odd sense of relief came over her.

Emma called up the stairs, "Breakfast is ready. We're eating outside, on the lanai this morning." Emma had set the table; glasses of orange juice and bowls of fruit were neatly arranged.

She caught Emma studying her. "There's something going on in that head of yours."

"Emma, I've decided to fly to California. There's no sense in putting it off any longer." *I've got to remember to call Steve and postpone dinner until after I return.*

#

The trip to California had been a roller coaster ride of emotions and long meetings with Kent's attorney, Ted Hawkins. The most difficult part of it all was packing up Kent's personal effects. His brother, Ian, should have received the boxes by now. She knew he'd be thankful for the family albums and baseball memorabilia.

Attorney Hawkins accommodated Allison's request to set up a substantial trust fund from an 'anonymous' benefactor for the

Dominguez children. She was gratified that he prioritized processing the paperwork before she returned to Florida.

CHAPTER FIFTY-FIVE

Dressed in sweat pants and a t-shirt, Allison pulled a Phil Bowie book off the shelf; he was one of her favorite writers, and curled up on the chaise in the library. She yelled a 'so-long' to Emma who was on her way to a Leading Ladies luncheon at the Ruth Eckerd Hall in Clearwater.

Engrossed in the story set in North Carolina, Allison was bothered when she had to set the book down and answer the doorbell. She couldn't believe her eyes—Kent's lover, Fernando Diez.

"What are you doing here?"

"Please, don't shut the door. I had to go through hell and back to find you."

"There is a little thing called privacy." She started to close the door. "Ever heard of it?"

"Stop! I swear I'll never contact you after this but, I must talk with you. Allison, let me come in. I promise I'll leave you in peace."

"Too late for that—don't you think?"

"All I need is fifteen minutes."

"You've got ten, Fernando. Make it quick!" There were no good manners squandered on him. The foyer was as far as she allowed him to enter.

"I'm not sure how or where to begin. I've gone over this

scenario a thousand times in my mind and now that I'm here—"

"You're down to nine minutes, so I suggest you say what you've come to say."

A piteously nervous Fernando reached into his jacket and removed an envelope.

He explained that he stopped by that day to hang out with Kent. He was pretty wasted when he arrived. They finished off a bottle of bourbon and watched porno flicks. Fernando came on to Kent.

"He had no idea I'm gay. No one on the team knows."

"Well, thank you for sharing, Fernando. I hope your purging makes your conscience feel better. Time's up. Now, get out!"

But a tearful Fernando started to speak.

"Don't say another word. I don't give a rat's ass about you or your disgusting excuse! You won't find absolution here!"

Fernando dropped the envelope on the hall table and left.

She slammed and bolted the door, picked up the envelope and walked to the couch were she collapsed.

It took time for Allison to regain her composure. She sat on the sofa and ran her fingers over the post-mark. Kent mailed the letter to Fernando the morning Kent was killed.

She tore it open with a vengeance. She stared at her husband's handwriting.

> *Fernando,*
> *By the time you read this letter I'll be gone. I can't stomach what I did. I'm ashamed of myself. I'm begging you, don't tell anybody what happened. The secret dies with me.*
> *I don't care if you're gay, but I'm not. Being drunk was no excuse. I just can't live with the guilt.*

You're a great athlete and a good friend. Allison is a special lady and I'm sure she'll never ruin either of our reputations.

I've thought this through, after I mail this letter, I'll sit down with a good bottle of bourbon then take care of business.

Next year, win the series.

Kent

"My, God, he was going to kill himself!" Weak in the knees, Allison walked to the credenza in the dining room, took out a large glass bowl, one of Mother's, and a pack of matches. She watched the letter burn to ashes.

CHAPTER FIFTY-SIX

The sound of Luciano Pavarotti singing <u>La donna e mobile</u> greeted Allison and Steve as they entered Maggiano's Restaurant. Steve checked her out in her little black dress. "You're a knockout tonight! Actually, I've never seen you prettier."

A bit early for their eight-thirty reservation, they waited at the bar and talked over drinks. He placed his hand over hers. His eyes locked with hers so deeply that she felt an overpowering closeness with him. He lifted her hand and pressed it lightly to his lips. A surge of excitement tingled in her belly.

"Oh, that's so Cary Grant!"

"I have a confession to make." He picked up his wine glass and sipped. "I wasn't sure you would take me up on my invitation."

"Sir," the maitre'd interrupted, "your table's ready. Please follow me." He escorted them to a quiet, candle-lit corner of the room. The atmosphere was perfect.

Allison paid close attention while Steve opened up about his college days at the University of Florida, studying anthropology. The university offered him a position in their North American Studies program which he seriously considered. But, after the serial killer, Danny Rolling, murdered the sister of one of his football teammates on the Gainesville campus, he was compelled to go into law enforcement.

By the time the waiter came to remove their empty appetizer plates and refill their wine glasses, she learned that Steve had married his college sweetheart, had no children, got divorced five years ago, and was born in St. Petersburg, Florida.

"Well, that's Steve DeMarcou in a nutshell. If you want to learn more, you'll have to go to dinner with me again."

"I may take you up on that offer."

An attractive, mature woman approached the table. "You're Allison Rogers!"

"I am," she answered. Steve pulled away to disengage himself from their conversation.

"I'm a big fan of Thomas Gunn and I love what you said about him on your show." She held out her cell phone and asked, "May I take a picture with you?"

Before Allison could answer, the lady handed Steve her phone. "Do you mind?" then leaned down and placed her arm around Allison and beamed for the camera. "Oh, thank you so much!" With a nod of approval at the picture on the screen, she turned and walked away.

"Did she say his name is Tommy Gunn?" Steve choked, "You've got to be kidding!"

"Poor thing." Allison chuckled. "What were his parents thinking?"

He leaned back. "It's obvious they weren't."

"But he is a good psychic. He's the one who led me to the pouches like the serial killer uses."

"Please, Allison. Can we talk about anything else? You know I'm not in to that psychic mumbo jumbo."

"Mumbo jumbo!" So much for the romantic mood.

"Sweetheart, you're beautiful, smart, and funny, and I like you, but it's the psychic thing that bites me."

"Then why'd you ask me what the stones meant?"

"That was my lieutenant's idea, not mine."

She lowered her voice. "A lot of well-respected agencies use psychics as investigative tools."

"I use sound, proven techniques, Allison—hard evidence."

"And, I've found exceptional psychics. It's sad you're too close-minded to consider anything that's not black or white."

"If you give me six winning lottery numbers, I'll reconsider and share the jackpot with you."

"Very funny."

"Aw come on, Allison. You people claim you can predict earthquakes and presidential assassinations and yet none of you can come up with five numbers and a Powerball number. Get real!"

"That's the final straw!" She leaned closer to him, out of earshot of the other patrons, not wanting to make a scene. "Steve, you're an arrogant ass!"

Allison stood, tossed her napkin on the table and the evening ended with a polite 'goodnight.' She excused herself, left the restaurant, and hailed a cab.

Allison was disappointed over her date with Steve and unable to sleep. She decided to get up and go over her notes for her lecture the next day. She went to her desk and picked up the file.

Half an hour later, the unopened file was still in her hand. Steve's charm, then his arrogance and ignorance played over in her mind.

Was the Universe trying to tell her she wasn't ready to date? Or was Steve just a jerk?

CHAPTER FIFTY-SEVEN

He read the notice in the newspaper, which advertised Allison Rogers' lecture at the Western Branch of the Clearwater Library.

"At last, we'll meet, Allison." He wanted to make a good first impression. He'd wear the suit he bought years ago but never wore.

She'll acknowledge me and smile. 'Thank you for your thoughtful flowers. We'll talk over a late lunch.'

He removed a heavily-scented bag from a chest in the back corner of the closet; unhooked the chain from around his neck for the first time in years, and dropped it into the pouch.

CHAPTER FIFTY-EIGHT

She stood at the podium aware of a man at the back of the room. He was dressed in a suit and tie but there was something odd about him that was unsettling. She squinted to see him more clearly, but the bright lights inhibited her vision.

For the first forty minutes, Allison talked about the benefits and pitfalls of psychic aptitude. As a general rule, the folks who attended her lectures were believers in the metaphysical but she felt it necessary to emphasize that they must keep a healthy dose of skepticism because anyone can be deceived.

She then told her enthusiastic, 'standing room only' audience, "We'll take a ten minute break and I'll return for questions."

The sound of applause welcomed her back to the lectern. The Q & A part of her lectures was her favorite because she enjoyed the interaction and feedback from her audience.

A lady in the front row raised her hand. "How do you know if your psychic is real?"

"Great question. A guideline to use is your common sense . . ."

The questions continued for thirty minutes and several hands remained raised.

"We're about out of time, so I'll take one more question."

The man in the suit raised his hand. He didn't wait to be called.

"I have a question about Karma," he politely stated from the back of the room.

Before Allison could answer him, a rotund woman seated toward the front of the room, sprung up and challenged, "I had my hand up first! Who do you think you are in that cheesy suit? Wait til I'm finished!"

Allison felt badly for the man, but answered the rude woman's question to avoid another outburst. She wanted to discuss the subject of Karma, but when she started to address him, he was gone.

Once the audience dispersed, Allison picked up her briefcase and started to leave when she was drawn to the area where the man had been.

A pouch on the chair! She dumped the contents into her hand. Allison knew what it meant, but she couldn't go back to Sergeant Vernon. Steve wasn't an option. Emma's admonishment to 'back off' was all she could do.

#

The sow humiliated him in front of Allison. *She spoiled everything!* He waited outside of the library consumed with rage. The fat pig exited the glass doors and waddled to her faded blue Hyundai. She squeezed her bulk behind the wheel.

She's alone—a good sign.

He put his car in gear and followed her into a nearby development. He waited until her front door closed before he stopped his car behind hers on the driveway. He reached under the front seat for what he needed and stepped out of his vehicle.

Miss Piggy answered the doorbell and squealed as the scalpel-sharp hunting knife slashed through her neck.

Her body fell in a heap like Jabba the Hutt. He kicked her puffy hand away so he could pull the door shut.

"Now you're finished, porky!"

CHAPTER FIFTY-NINE

It had been weeks since the incident after the library. There was no good Karma that came from killing Miss Piggy, but there was satisfaction—better than joy; better than peace. Joy was a temporary high; peace was a state of mind that he couldn't maintain. Satisfaction—now that was new. It lasted and kept his demons away. He was content.

There was no need to tell Anne about Allison or what happened after the library. He would make the decisions from now on. All Anne would have to concern herself with was his happiness. Like dear old dad quoted to mom a million times, "A virtuous woman is a crown to her husband."

Each night he would fantasize that Anne lay next to him in bed so he could read their book of poetry aloud to her. And after he turned out the light, he'd wait for her to say, "That special place between two souls, where only we can go," and then they would say 'good night.'

H.O.K. set two places for breakfast, as was his new habit, and imagined what it would be like to share every day with her. After he cleared their dishes and tidied the kitchen, he went to the cabinet and took out the project file.

An hour had passed by the time he had organized his plans. He creased a slip of paper in half, and placed it in the folder with the others.

#

H.O.K. cruised through one shit-hole town after another and scouted the countryside to find the perfect location. Plenty of places would do, but he wanted a sign.

It took all day to find what he sought; in the middle of nowhere, a rusted mailbox with faded letters. A-D-A-M-S. It leaned against an old wire fence. A deserted ram-shackled house and barn sat far back from the road.

CHAPTER SIXTY

For the past three nights Allison had been haunted by the same recurrent dream, waking before it finished. In the stillness of the room, she concentrated. The particulars came back in pieces.

She wrote the fragmented details of her dream on the paper she kept on the nightstand.

- A factory, white smoke billowed from tall smoke stacks
- A nondescript voice repeated 'Help me'
- Decrepit house, smells of urine, beehives
- Three stones

She knew the dream was important, but none of it made sense.

She rubbed her sleep-deprived eyes and reviewed the list in her mind. Then it came to her. The smoke stacks!

"It's the phosphate plant off State Road 60! I've passed there a hundred times!"

She dressed, and after a quick cup of coffee, took off in her car. She was on her way to Polk County.

#

The sun streamed through the hole in the roof of the old

building. The promise of a new day brought by the golden rays contrasted the horror of the bizarre scene below.

The Hand of Karma stoked the white hot coals and held the rod in the glowing embers.

"Who are you?" The man screamed, "Why are you doing this?" His head was secured to a vertical support beam. Bands of silver tape wrapped around his body. His shoulders and chest were bound tight; wrists pressed to his hips; fingers turned blue. His face contorted. He resembled a live totem pole that gasped and struggled.

H.O.K. moved closer to the totem, and, with the glowing red end of the poker, pressed it into the flesh of the man's exposed thigh.

"WHY?" the man screamed.

"Still enjoy the smell of burnt flesh?"

"I'll do anything you ask," he sobbed. "I can get you money." The screams continued. "Don't do this!" he begged.

The Hand of Karma returned the poker to the pail and stirred the hot coals.

#

Allison drove up and down the two-lane highway in the area of the phosphate plant, paying attention to every building. And then, she saw it! The abandoned tenant house. The half collapsed barn. Dead tree in the front yard. And, the abandoned bee hives. The same as the dream.

She drove a few yards past a gravel lane that ran alongside the abandoned property and parked in front of the rusted wire gate surrounding the house. Allison surveyed the area and saw no cars and no people. She slipped her cell phone in her pocket, then got out of the car, squeezed through the wire gate, and ignored the 'No Trespassing' sign.

She arrived at the open front door and found it was held onto the frame by one hinge.

"Hello? Anybody here?" she hollered, then pushed the door

open so she could press through.

The cluttered floor was covered with empty Sterno cans, old food packages, and piles of rags.

"Is someone here?" she called out.

She found a broken chair leg she could use to protect herself, if necessary.

The stench of stale urine turned her stomach. She cupped her hand over her nose and moved to another room. The room was smaller and must have belonged to a child at one time. Sections of the faded cowboy print wallpaper peeled away from the walls. Graffiti had been spray painted over the happy faces of young cowboys riding their steeds.

Allison walked through the house and had to step over remnants of broken furniture and trash, avoiding holes in the rotten floor boards.

Déjà vu.

She moved to the back of the house, reached a closed door and gave it a push.

"Holy crap!"

A big gray cat darted past her. She lost her balance and fell back onto a broken crate. Her sweat pants tore and her elbow banged on the floor.

"Stupid cat!"

#

The poker was ready. It was pressed into the totem's cheek until it burned through to the inside his mouth. The screams stopped when he passed out. The smell of roasted flesh filled the barn.

"Time to wake up," H.O.K. whispered, then splashed water on him. "The only way to salvation is to pay your debt ten times over." Three stones were dropped at the feet of the totem.

H.O.K. kicked over the pail of hot coals and emptied the last of the accelerant over the dry straw. He tossed the empty can into the flames as he walked out of the building.

#

The view from the back of the house revealed little more than an unattended field and a barn that leaned precariously to one side. *What am I missing?* Allison had no answer, but searched the house one more time before she left.

Half-way down the lane on her way to her car, she spun around at the sound of a vehicle that sped up the gravel road behind her. It came from the barn! She dove beside a large tree as the car sped by; too fast to see the driver. A black car!

Zapped by a rush of adrenaline, she bolted toward the barn.

A rusted skeleton of an old tractor, entangled in a mass of overgrown weeds, pressed against the leaning structure. She climbed onto it and attempted to peek in the window but couldn't see through the thick filth that coated the inside of the panes of glass. She smelled SMOKE!

She got down from her position and dialed 9-1-1.

Someone screamed from inside, "Help! Help me!"

She raced to the front of the barn. Thick corroded chains held the weathered doors closed. Frantic, she ran around the side and discovered a partially opened stall door.

FLAMES! "My God!"

"Help me!" The cries became more frantic.

Thick black smoke burned her throat and stung her eyes. She gasped for air as she ran toward the cry and found the grotesque sight. She groped at the bonds that held him. They didn't give.

So hot. Can't breathe.

She drew in deep breaths. Her head throbbed.

"Well, hello there." His voice was comforting. "Keep breathing that oxygen. You took in some smoke! You're on your way to Brandon Regional Hospital."

Someone whispered, "Imagine the coroner's face when she sees the other one."

CHAPTER SIXTY-ONE

Polk County, Florida: Local television personality, Allison Rogers, is being called a hero for her attempt to rescue a man from a burning building. She called 9-1-1 when she saw smoke coming from an abandoned building off Highway 60 in Bartow and entered the barn when she heard cries for help. Once inside, she found a man bound to a support beam who appeared to have been tortured. She was unable to free him. Ms. Rogers was taken to Brandon Regional Hospital suffering from smoke inhalation and minor injuries.

The man was pronounced dead at the scene. His mutilated body has been positively identified as that of former college professor, Adam Langley, who was sentenced to prison in 1994 and recently released. Langley was convicted of false imprisonment and aggravated battery on his student and lover, Kim Loudernal after he disfigured her by using a soldering iron. Langley was also a person of interest in the disappearance of two other students, Crystal March and Sarah

Greenwald, who remain missing.

Evidence found at the scene has led police to suspect there may be a link between Langley's murder and the stone killings.

"Christl!" Anne threw the newspaper across the room. "What have you done?"

CHAPTER SIXTY-TWO

Satisfied with his choice to release Adam Langley's damned soul, H.O.K. had graduated and no longer needed his teacher. It was he who held them accountable, not her. From now on, he would decide which soul needed cleansing. He wouldn't wait for her to beckon him.

"This calls for a letter to my beloved parents." In his journal he wrote:

> *Dear Mom and Dad,*
> *Today I feel great! I am enlightened. I am The Hand of Karma. This is how it works. Everything you do comes back on you, good or bad. If you don't live long enough in this lifetime, it'll get you in the next. I'd hate to be you when you come back.*
> *Your Devoted Son, H.O.K.*

The sun shown in the kitchen window through the louvers that were kept closed most of the time. But this morning, he let in the light. It was warm and soothing. He felt a sense of peace.

After a hearty breakfast, and two cups of coffee, he read the paper. For the first time in years, he didn't turn on the television.

He left the kitchen sparkling clean and headed for the shower.

He stood under the hot water until it ran cold. It took that long to rid himself of the last vestige of smoke that permeated his hair and skin.

Inside his walk-in closet, he searched through the drab colors he usually wore until he found the long-sleeved silk print shirt he'd bought during a rare high time and had never worn. It fit his mood. He buttoned his sleeves at the wrist and checked his image in the mirror.

"Allison," he asked out loud, "why did you come? I almost ran you down! How did you know where to find me?" None of that mattered. It was meant to be. Every cell in his body was filled with gratitude to the Universe that he hadn't run her over or hurt her. It defied all logic, but she was there at the farm.

"Well, my dear friend, allow me to reciprocate."

It was a powerful need he had to establish a meaningful dialogue with her. He wanted her to know that her presence at the barn validated their kinship. His life now had meaning and she would want to know that he was enlightened.

"All in good time, Allison."

CHAPTER SIXTY-THREE

The tension between the sisters was palpable. It was the worst argument they'd ever had. Allison understood the worry and stress she'd caused her sister, but for Emma to call her out in front of the doctor and nurses at the hospital was wrong.

The hurt caused by her sister's remarks made it impossible for Allison to stay in the house. She carried her suitcase to the front door.

"Where're you going now?" Emma asked in an authoritative tone. "You just got out of the hospital."

"To a hotel!"

"Why?"

"After what you said to me . . .?"

"Allison, we're all we have. We have to protect each other. What you did was insane! What were you doing there, anyway?"

"I was doing research."

"Well, your research almost got you killed—twice! That damn book's not worth it! This nonsense has got to stop!"

Before Allison could say another word, Emma started to cry. Allison had never seen her sister this irate before and didn't know how to respond. She reached out to touch her but Emma pulled away.

"If your work means more to you than I do, then go!" Emma

turned and stormed out of the room.

Allison stood in stunned silence for as long as it took for the sound of the slamming door to her sister's bedroom to reverberate through the house.

#

From a distance he saw the garage door open. Allison wiped her cheek and appeared to be crying. He watched her place a suitcase in the trunk of her car and drive off.

#

Pelicans flew above her car as she drove over the Belleair Causeway to the beach. The beautiful clear day and warm breeze off the gulf didn't stop the hurt rising from her core. She knew Emma was trying to protect her. She knew Emma was afraid for her. But how could her sister not understand the importance of what she was doing?

"Dammit, if I can help take this maniac off the streets, I will. I don't need her permission."

After she settled into her room at the Sheraton Sand Key, she opened the balcony doors and took in a deep breath of the salty air. Her chest still ached. Was it the smoke she inhaled at the barn that caused the pain or her fight with Emma? Tears rose, followed by anger. The one person she could always count on had just slammed the door on her.

A child's antics on the beach below caught her attention. Seagulls soared around the little boy who screamed with delight as he fed pieces of bread to them, and for a few moments her thoughts were lost in the frenzied scene.

Allison wiped the tears from her cheeks and stepped back into her room. She wouldn't feel sorry for herself. This wasn't about her. This wasn't the time to lick her wounds. She knew she was close to tying the loose ends together and absolutely sure she could stop the next murder. She made the call.

#

"Thanks for taking my call, Steve. I didn't know where else to turn." She sensed his scrutiny.

"You said it was urgent, Allison. What's this about?"

"I need your help." She described what she'd heard when she went to the Crestview scene. She told him how she went to the St. Petersburg Police Department.

"Yeah, I heard all about it."

With all the trust she could muster, she told him about the nightmares, how she found the man in the barn, that she lied to the police and said when she drove by she saw the smoke, and how she was almost run down by a dark car leaving the scene.

"It's all fitting together Steve, and if you let me have a look at the crime scene photos—"

"Allison, I can't do that, and it's wrong for you to ask!"

"Dammit to Hell! I've worked with police departments before. Why can't I get anyone here to pay attention?"

"Allison, I know you're well-intended, but do you know how many calls we get from people calling themselves psychics and how much effort we put into following up on those leads? It takes valuable time away from a homicide investigation. And for the most part, they give us public knowledge just like you gave.

"Why can't you let this go, Allison and put all these stories in your book? It'll make for good reading."

"This is NOT about my book! It's about stopping a killer. And if you won't help, I'll find someone who will!"

#

Pride aside, Allison called Anne Preston asking for her help.

"You've piqued my curiosity, Allison. I'm eager to learn what I can do for YOU. From what I see on your television reports, you're doing just fine."

In true 'Allison' fashion she charged ahead, knowing that Anne was somehow connected to the killer. She informed Anne that she was close to identifying the Stone Killer and was certain that Anne could confirm what Allison already knew and fill in the missing blanks.

Anne questioned why Allison was so involved. She had no choice but to reveal to Anne that initially she started to receive images of the murders. Soon after, the killer tried to contact her. Allison emphasized that whoever it is may have a direct connection to Anne.

"Where is all of this going, Allison? Did you go to the police?"

"Yes, but they gave no credence to what I had to offer."

"Then, why are you so interested in this case?"

"As you know, Anne, my husband died recently. I knew he was in some terrible danger but I was too late with my warnings. I don't want that to happen again. I wasn't able to stop Kent's murder, but I can stop this killer from hurting another person."

"If you couldn't prevent your husband's murder, you most likely will not be able to stop it from happening to a stranger. However, you did ask me to verify a few facts. I can at least do that much. Why don't you tell me what you know." Anne reached for the Baccarat crystal paperweight. "We can work on it together."

Allison ignored the sappy sweet offer of 'together' as well as her condescending tone. She detailed all that she knew and stated, "Everyone knows about the stones found at the scenes, but it's what they're in that's important."

"Why does that matter?"

"It led me to you, Anne."

"What are you suggesting?"

"I believe the killer may be someone you know!"

"Preposterous! Absolutely not!"

"Anne, you give out pouches with stones and crystals in them."

"A lot of readers give them to their clients." Anne turned the crystal paperweight over in her hand. "I offer them as needed." Anne sighed. "Why do I need to justify what I do, to you?"

Allison feigned an apology. "I thought we were working together."

"Yes, of course. Please continue."

"In the course of my research, I learned that the pouches left at the murders are identical to those that you use."

"They may be similar."

"No! They're identical. They are specifically scented for you!"

No response from Anne.

"One of your clients is a murderer! We can stop him!"

Anne tightened her grip around the cool, smooth crystal. "Do you not think if one of them was a murderer that I wouldn't know?"

Frustration seethed through Allison. "My point is I believe he wants me to know who he is. He sent flowers to me, written notes, and he attended one of my lectures. He asked me about Karma."

"You've seen him?" Anne's hand flew to her mouth.

Allison said that she wasn't able to make out his features and that it was no accident that he left one of her pouches with a Jewish Star in it on his chair.

"Rubbish! The killer's not Jewish. Your guy at the lecture is obviously NOT the killer! It was most certainly a prank."

Allison shifted in her chair. "It didn't feel like a prank."

"You said he drives a dark car—Allison, you're one hundred percent wrong! That's not what I see. He drives a light-colored four-door truck with an Ohio license plate."

"Anne, you're involved whether you like it or not! You may not want to believe me, but you're connected to him!"

"I hardly think so, however since you insist I'll go through my Rolodex. It won't be necessary for you to contact me again. Should I discover anything of importance, I'll ring you up. And Allison, the pouch with stones I left for you when we had lunch at the E&E

Restaurant were to help you over your emotional distress. Please take advantage of its power. And now, if you'll excuse me, I have a very busy schedule." Anne hung up.

Allison sat back in her chair and said to herself, "Anne, my psychic friend, you are one crafty liar and as far as your thoughtful 'gift' . . . you already knew that I gave the pouch and stones to Sergeant Vernon."

CHAPTER SIXTY-FOUR

Allison was frustrated, bone-tired, and alone. Twenty-four hours of undisturbed sleep is what she needed. But first, she had to get aspirin for her headache. She'd buy them at the hotel gift shop.

The elevator doors opened into the lobby. "Emma!" She hurried over, arms outstretched. "I'm so sorry."

"It wasn't your fault." Emma embraced her. "I'm the one who should—"

"Forget it. Let's not ever do that again!"

They sat in the lounge wiping away tears, unashamed by the spectacle they made.

"How'd you know where I'd be?"

"It's your favorite weekend getaway and restaurant. Since we're here . . ." They talked on their way to the dining room. "A table by the window, please."

A bottle of wine and dinner finished, they devoured their Double Death by Chocolate dessert and watched the sunset. Emma beamed when Allison told her she was right about so many things and that she decided to give up the television reporting.

The server returned and handed Allison a folded note. "A gentleman who was sitting at that table asked me to deliver this."

Allison remembered the handwriting. *A fountain pen.* She

turned. "Where is he?"

"He asked me to wait until after he left to give it to you."

"He's here, Emma," she whispered.

"Who's here?"

Allison turned to the waiter, "Do you remember what he looked like?"

"I don't know—just an average guy."

"Did he sign a receipt?"

"He paid with cash and left a big tip!" The young man stepped back. "Will there be anything else?"

"No, thank you." Allison waited until he moved away from the table to read the note.

"Allison, you look like you've seen a ghost."

She handed the paper to Emma.

> *Dear Allison,*
> *Thank you for coming to the farm. Couldn't believe I saw you. I wanted to thank you in person. Sorry it didn't work out this time.*
> *Your Devoted Friend, H.O.K.*

"Oh, sweet Jesus! Allison, you're coming home with me right now!"

"You won't get an argument out of me!"

Emma motioned to the waiter for the check, only to discover that their bill was paid by the man who sent the note.

"That's it!" Emma stood. "We're going now!"

They left the dining room and hurried toward the elevator.

"Allison, we need an escort and I don't want any flack. I'm not getting into that elevator or your room without one!"

"Of course we do! Just the thought of that cretin sitting so close to us and then buying us dinner . . . makes me want to throw up."

#

Crouched behind a potted palm tree near the concierge desk, he watched Allison walk past him. What did he just hear? Her words cut deep. He thought she was his friend . . .

#

"Excuse me, sir?" Emma called to the burly, thirty-something security guard walking through the lobby. "I just saw my crazy ex-husband here. Will you escort us to our room?"

"Yes, ma'am. He bothering you?"

"Not yet. I just want to be prudent." Protection in tow, they rode the elevator in silence. The doors opened to the fifth floor. Security stepped out first.

"Its room five twenty-seven," Allison said, and waited for him to lead the way.

"Ladies, if you'll wait over there," he pointed down the hall, "I'll check it out for you."

Allison handed him her key.

"Allison, we've got to call the police!"

"A lot of good that'll do. What can I tell them—I got another fan letter?"

"It's different now. He's following you!"

"How can we prove it? What did he do—leave me a note—pay for our dinner?"

"Aren't you scared?"

"Of course, I am. But right now, I want to go home."

"All clear," the guard announced.

"You checked everywhere, right?" Emma asked.

"Even the balcony, ma'am."

"Thank you. We're checking out now. Can you wait?"

"Yes ma'am. I'll be right here in the hallway."

Both door locks secured behind them, Emma opened the armoire and tossed Allison's things onto the bed. Allison opened her luggage on the stand and stuffed the clothes into it. Toiletries from the bathroom were dumped into an overnight bag.

Ten minutes later the door opened. The stoic security guard said, "That's gotta be a record." He told them he'd radioed the front desk and since they didn't have extra room charges, they could go right out. "The valet will bring your cars around."

Even their capable escort couldn't alleviate the unease Allison felt as they waited under the hotel's canopy.

#

H.O.K. watched Allison talking to the security guard while she waited for her car.

He stayed until her vehicle disappeared down the street. He felt dejected, like a fan waiting for an autograph and blown off by the celebrity.

On his way home, he thought of the blade in the cabinet. He remembered his promise not to cut anymore, a promise he knew he wouldn't keep. The burning slice into his flesh would be his only relief from this humiliation.

"Allison, why would you let your sister insult me that way?"

The ritual done, he bandaged his forearm. He needed to sleep and reached for the last of his Seconal. This should do the job.

He knocked over his alarm clock when he answered the phone.

"Hello," he slurred.

"What the bloody hell are you doing?"

He cleared his throat, attempting to speak, but her irate voice fired one question after another.

"Notes and flowers? Why did you go to her lecture? Why did you leave that?"

He tried to explain that he only wanted to meet her, that he knew she'd understand and approve of his actions, that she, too, was a hand of Karma.

"Are you bloody daft?" the shrill voice demanded.

He propped up on his elbows, felt the wetness on his bandage. His wound had begun to bleed again. He knew he was careless last night and sliced too deep. His arm ached. His head ached. His heart ached.

"It was all very innocent."

Silence.

"Hello? Anne, are you there?" The buzzing on the line told him she'd hung up. It felt as if the air in the room had been sucked out. The walls closed in on him. His mind raced.

"What the fuck was that all about?" It dawned on him. "You must've thought that I was pursuing Allison Rogers because I wanted her!" He chalked up Anne's anger to jealousy. The thought of that was so intense, he got hard.

Once he relieved his sexual tension, he ruminated about the deeds he'd performed over the last several months. She must have been admiring his skills and bravery to say nothing of his ingenuity for clearing the scum off of the pond.

He picked up the well-worn book of poetry and spoke the title aloud. "Knowing." The book rested on his chest as he contemplated the notion that if she could become jealous, that was his sign.

She loves me.

CHAPTER SIXTY-FIVE

"Well, good morning Sunshine," he said. "You hung up last night before I could clarify my friendship with Allison Rogers."

She held the phone away from her ear with disgust, chiding herself for not checking the caller I.D.

"What do you want, Elliott?"

"I need to see you today."

"Today? That would be impossible. I'm extremely busy." She rubbed the Baccarat crystal paperweight on her desk. "I can see you the day after tomorrow."

His lips tightened until the vermillion border turned white.

"Didn't you hear me, sweetheart? It's imperative that I see you today!"

"I heard you. I'm not sure I like your familiarity."

"Anne, don't treat me like I'm one of your insignificant clients. We both know I'm much more than that."

Without responding to his statement and provoked with his attitude she shuffled papers on her desk and made him wait. "I've just checked. I can squeeze you in at the end of my day tomorrow. Be here at six. But, do understand, I can't give you much time."

"Squeeze me in? Who do you think I am?"

She hung up on him.

"Sweetheart?" she coughed. "I know precisely who you are Elliott and you have gone TOO far."

Anne opened her umbrella and dashed to the coffee shop across the street. Her shoes and legs were wet from the puddles she couldn't avoid, but a mug of freshly brewed coffee would warm her.

People darted into the shop seeking shelter from the unexpected downpour. She waited in line still irritated by his presumption—SWEETHEART! *You festering hemorrhoid!*

Customers were distracted by the game show on the old television set bracketed on the ceiling. Conversations stopped when they heard:

> BREAKING NEWS! Ray Castrovic, boyfriend of murder victim Jennifer Barrett, has been charged with the sexual assault and murder of her eight-year-old daughter Kelly Barrett. In a written statement today, Castrovic confessed to the murder of the child. He has not been charged in the death of Jennifer Barrett, the child's mother, and vehemently denies any involvement in Jennifer's murder.
>
> Stay tuned for further updates.

A bolt of fear struck Anne.

CHAPTER SIXTY-SIX

The clock read five forty-five. He wasn't due until six. She removed the taser from her desk drawer and slid it into her pocket. Anne jolted when Elliott stormed into her office early and unannounced.

"Quite an entrance you've made. I don't recall you knocking. But now that you're here, be seated."

"I don't want to sit!" He paced.

She seated herself at her desk creating a barrier between them. "What was so imperative that you couldn't wait see me?"

"Anne," he stammered, "I had something important to tell you, and you made me wait!"

"And, YOU broke the rules when you killed an innocent woman!"

"That fat pig wasn't innocent."

Anne struggled to keep her composure. His lunacy was far worse than she anticipated. How had she lost control of him and how many others have there been?

"I'm speaking of Jennifer Barrett."

"Jennifer Barrett? She wasn't innocent! She killed her daughter. She cut her head off and—"

"Elliott! You arrogant oaf! She didn't kill her; her bloody low-life boyfriend did. He confessed! He killed the girl!"

Elliott leaned over the desk.

"But, I did what you told me," his voice cracked, "make the guilty pay."

"Elliott, you didn't abide by our arrangement. I didn't tell you that Jennifer Barrett was guilty. You took it upon yourself, and herein lies the problem—YOU!" She pointed toward the door. "I can't help you with your Karma anymore."

"Anne, because of your guidance, my Karma's clear. I'm strong. I can make the decisions for both of us."

"This ends now! There will be no more contact. I can no longer allow you to contaminate my life with your malignant energy!"

"You can't just discard me!" He pounded the desk. "I WON'T LET YOU!"

"You won't let me? How dare you!" She put her hand on the crystal paperweight.

"What are you going to do with that?" he sneered. "Hit me?"

"You sicken me, Elliott. Get out!"

"Anne, you don't mean what you're saying. It's your jealousy talking. You're just insecure about my friendship with Allison Rogers, but she doesn't mean anything to me. She's no threat to us!"

"Are you insane? There is no US!"

"Of course there is—we're bound by the secrets we share."

"Elliott, this conversation is over!" Anne stood and placed her hand in her pocket. "I want you to leave!"

He backed away from the desk and walked to the door. "You need me, Anne, I know you do!" He closed the door.

The lock set behind him. Something crashed against the door.

"You pathetic bastard," she called after him, "you don't know me!"

He needed to escape her words, yet had to will his legs to move one step at a time until he reached his car.

"How could she say that?" His tingling fingers fumbled with his keys, barely able to start the car. "How could she forget the poetry—

the nights she came to me when I slept and how she pleasured me while I dreamed?" His mind was as numb as his hands. He arrived home remembering little of the drive from her office.

It had been hours since he returned from his disastrous meeting with her. Contrary to his normal habit, he remained in his clothes and sat motionless on the sofa. The only sound in the dark room came from his breathing in and out, in and out.

A lifetime of rejections ran through his mind. And now, Anne's words—"There is no us!"

He called repeatedly. He could convince her if she'd only give him a chance to explain.

"Remember Anne—mine to give, yours to keep, only the two of us know; that special place between two souls, where only we can go."

He poured the last of the scotch into his glass from his mother's Waterford decanter. He remembered watching how carefully she placed her precious crystal in the china cabinet. She protected it more than she did me.

He pressed the redial button.

"Anne, I'm sorry. I made a mistake. Don't spoil what we have. Please pick up."

Minutes later, "Call me now, Anne. I know you're there. I'm waiting."

His next message: "You're acting like a child. This isn't over and I will call until you pick up!"

By the seventeenth unanswered call, blood pulsed hard through the veins in his neck; he paced from room to room, streams of sweat drizzled down his spine.

"Stop jerking me around," his tone more demanding. "Karma is the tie that binds us. Get it, Anne—US."

He waited a half hour and tried again. This time his number was blocked.

"Do you really think that's going to stop me, Anne?" he screamed.

He finished his glass of scotch and reached for another. "Fuck!" He smashed the empty decanter onto the bar. Tiny shards of glass flew into his face. Without regard to the trickles of blood, he drove to the all-night gas station close to his home. He called Anne from the pay phone. This time the connection went through, but she didn't speak.

"Anne, don't hang up. I don't want to disappoint you. I want to make you happy."

"I've received enough of your 'charming' messages. Don't ring me again. Goodbye, Elliott."

He dropped the receiver. "Anne," he whispered, "I love you."

The varoom of a motorcycle that pulled up next to him vibrated in his chest.

"Buddy, you okay?"

He spun around and saw a burly man straddling the bike; a woman sat behind him, concern showed on her face. "Hey man, your face is bleeding."

With no acknowledgment, he walked away.

CHAPTER SIXTY-SEVEN

Sleep evaded him. Thoughts of women he dated years ago taunted him. He cringed remembering Ruthie Levine and the crush he had on her. He was humiliated when she left the prom with someone else. He returned home dejected. The next time he saw her was at his parents' funeral and she was very pregnant.

The occasional girlfriends he had in college often criticized him for his over-zealous attempts at sex, called him clumsy and ineffective. They didn't give him a chance.

Prostitutes weren't nit-picky. They didn't need to be charmed.

He sat upright in bed. "How could I have been so stupid? Anne's not like the whores. No more charging at her like a bull in a china shop. I need to be gentle and romantic."

The flower shop opened at nine and already people bustled in and out. Refrigerated cases were lined up against the side wall. So much to choose from, but no red roses. Revolting. Too much like my dearly departed parents' funeral. He chose yellow, white, and coral roses; a dozen of each. She'll know how awful I feel about my thoughtless behavior and see how sorry I am.

"Shall I add a little more baby's breath, Sir?"

"No, thank you. This will do the trick," and he left the store with his precious cargo.

#

Anne enjoyed having coffee on her balcony and now that a storm had blown past, the air off the Gulf seemed to smell particularly salty. A schooner sailed over the clear blue water; seagulls soared; a lone swimmer splashed in the surf.

Seated on the lounge chair, she dropped her calendar on her lap and sipped the steaming brew. The daunting task awaited her attention.

She dialed number after number and left the same scripted message for each client, grateful when she didn't have to speak to them directly. Only two people answered.

"This is Anne Preston. I find it necessary to cancel your upcoming appointment as I will be out of the country for the month of March. My dear mum will be having hip replacement surgery. I will ring you up when I return. Thank you for your understanding."

She closed her datebook. "I hate you for this, Elliott!"

#

Elliott carried the vase of flowers in the cardboard container and placed them on the front seat of his car, careful not to disturb a single petal and drove to her office. He arrived before Anne as planned.

The offering was placed outside of her door. He adjusted a piece of baby's breath the accommodating salesgirl had added to the arrangement and repositioned the card.

> *Dear Anne,*
>
> *Please forgive my brutish behavior. We've wasted so much time; let's make up for it now. Mine to give, Yours to keep –*
>
> *Love, Elliott*

He left the building and stepped into the shadow of the portico in time to see her arrive.

His excitement was barely containable. Still he waited for her to read his note and digest his apology. Then, he'd make his move.

#

She arrived at her office still filled with contempt for the presumptuous prick that forced her to disrupt her life.

A cloud of uneasiness surrounded her as she approached the building. At the entranceway, she stepped into an ice cold vortex. Her pace quickened as she turned into the corridor toward her office and halted when she saw what greeted her.

Anne removed the card. "You're beyond delusional!" Several pieces of baby's breath fell from the bouquet as she snatched the vase off the floor and retraced her steps out of the building. Sure he was watching, she paused for effect, stood in front of the dumpster and raised the vase over her head.

"I don't want your bloody flowers you wretched clod!" and jammed them into the receptacle.

She brushed her hands off as if washing away the entire incident.

#

Aghast at what he'd just witnessed, he grabbed at his chest, willing his heart not to explode from the pain.

"You can't still be mad at me, Anne," he cried aloud. Shaking with hurt then trembling with rage, he lingered in the shadows until he composed himself enough to escape to his car not sure of what to do or where to go.

Then he thought of Allison, his only friend. She'll know what to do.

He pictured himself sitting in her lovely living room. She would offer him a glass of homemade lemonade and listen attentively to

THE HAND OF KARMA

him as he bared his soul to her.

> *Allison, please tell me what I should do.*
> *She would say: You dear, sweet soul. You don't deserve this.*
> *I would say: But I've tried so hard.*
> *She would say: Elliott, you've done everything right. I know Anne loves you.*
> *I would say: She ruined my flowers.*
> *She would say: Elliott, she's playing hard to get. She wants to be pursued.*
> *Write her a romantic letter and put it in a beautiful card.*

"Great idea, Allison! I knew you'd have the answer." He put his car in gear and drove away.

"I won't forget you, Allison."

#

Parked at the far end of the lot, he slouched behind the steering wheel. The Toyota was partially obscured by the dumpster, where yesterday she destroyed his flowers. Even with the windows down, the temperature in the car was stifling. He undid his collar button and cuffs.

His shirt was soaked through by the time she made her appearance. She stopped to talk to a delivery man who pushed a dolly stacked with packages.

"Why are you flirting with him?" He gripped the steering wheel until his hands were numb. "Don't you know you belong to me?"

As she walked across the asphalt, Anne seemed lost in pleasant thought. His heart fluttered with excitement when she approached her car and reached beneath the windshield wiper for the pink envelope. This would make her happy.

He watched in agonizing astonishment as she tore it into little pieces!

She didn't even fucking read it!

"Stop playing hard to get! You know how this hurts me!" He started to sweat. His cheeks burned. "This is the last straw, Anne. I became the Hand of Karma for us! This is the way you treat me for all I've done? You're making me angry." He pounded the dashboard until it cracked.

She pulled onto the highway. The Toyota tailed her car maintaining a safe distance. "You'd best be going straight home and I'd better not see that delivery man sniffing around."

The BMW turned into the gated complex; he slowed down and watched her park. A quick U-turn and he was in the lot across the street tucked behind landscaping. She couldn't leave without him knowing.

The early evening sky glowed pink and red, like a halo around her building. *Isn't it nice sharing this beautiful sunset, Anne?*

"What are you doing, love," he asked aloud, "sitting on your bed, slipping off your shoes? Off comes your suit. First, your jacket. Then, your skirt and blouse."

His eyes closed and continued his fantasy.

"It's getting late." He pictured her naked outside the shower, testing the water temperature before she got in.

"Oh, Anne, you're all soapy. Are your nipples hard for me? You know I'm watching you, baby." He squirmed slightly to adjust himself for his growing erection.

"You smell so sweet."

TAP, TAP, TAP!

Startled, he jumped and saw a deputy sheriff staring at him.

"Excuse me, sir." The deputy leaned forward. "Is everything all right?"

"Yeah, sure," Elliott replied.

"You were parked here for a pretty long time. I thought there might be something wrong."

"Nothing's wrong, officer."

"Mind if I take a look at your identification?" the deputy asked nonchalantly.

Struck by fear, Elliott opened the console to retrieve the registration and pushed the chamois pouch deep into the compartment. He fumbled for his driver's license and handed both to the deputy.

"Thank you, sir." The deputy shined his flashlight on the driver's license and registration then returned them to Elliott. There was no cause to run them through the computer.

"I came to watch the sunset. Guess I fell asleep." Elliott saw the clock on the dashboard. "Eight o'clock? I should be getting home."

The deputy stood there too long for Elliott's comfort.

"Yes, Sir. Drive safely."

Inside the patrol car, the overhead light remained on. The officer spoke into his radio.

What's he saying? Did he see it?

Elliott started his car. "Goodnight, Anne." That fucking cop had to ruin our night together!

He waved and nodded at the deputy who made eye contact when he drove past.

CHAPTER SIXTY-EIGHT

Allison sipped a glass of juice while she sat by the pool soaking in the morning sun. The fragrance of citrus blossoms from the nearby grove filled the air.

Psychic investigations done; her manuscript completed; one last thing to do before this god-awful year was behind her. It was nine-thirty. She didn't have to meet Emma at the Pinellas County State Attorney's office until two. She dreaded rehashing the details of the night she was attacked, but keeping Armando Tiberi, Madame Marie's son locked up would be worth it.

As disinclined as she was to leave the peaceful surroundings, she forced herself out of the chair and went into the house to prepare for her day. Halfway up the staircase there was a thud at the front door. Still in her bathrobe, she put her eye to the peephole in time to see the mail truck pull away.

#

He saw the front door open. She stepped outside wearing her robe and slippers, picked up the newspaper, and walked to the mailbox and opened it.

Satisfied she'd find what he'd left for her; he started the engine and drove away.

#

She gathered the mail and turned, half expecting to see someone standing behind her. What she saw was a kid on a skateboard checking her out.

"I'm standing here in my robe and big fuzzy slippers! What a sight I must be for the neighbors."

On her approach to the front of the house, she saw it taped to the door and gasped when she saw the bright blue ink on the envelope!

She ripped it off the wood, rushed inside, bolted the door, and set the alarm.

With trembling hands, she opened it.

> *My Dearest Friend,*
>
> *The night I bought you dinner your sister called me a cretin. It took a lot of effort, but I finally have forgiven you for not defending me. I wanted you to know that.*
>
> *I'm sad to learn that your work at the station is finished. We do a lot of good, you and I.*
>
> *You will be happy to know that I have been rewarded for my deeds and I find it necessary to end our relationship as I am starting on a new journey.*
>
> *Kindred Souls Forever,*
>
> *H.O.K.*

She re-read the letter; her thoughts flashed back to Tropicana Field and Lenny Chambers. One by one, each murder replayed in her mind. What difference had her abilities made? NOT A DAMN THING. She was over it. Emma was right; let the police do their job.

Allison struggled with who she was and what being psychic had done to her life. Kent was killed. No one wanted her help. She almost died.

She would live without using her sixth sense. Her life was calm now. For the first time in a long while, she was content.

Allison tore the note into pieces and dropped them in the trash

CHAPTER SIXTY-NINE

H.O.K. turned off his computer, satisfied with the recipe he found for chloroform and amazed at the ease with which it could be researched on the internet. It would only be viable for a few hours after it was mixed. He would have to be precise with his plan.

Wired even after he watched the late night news, he washed down a couple of sleeping pills with scotch. He climbed into bed, closed his eyes, and thought of Anne.

The scent of the perfume she wore lingered on the pillow he sprayed and now clutched in his arms. It was Anne he held. She kissed him, fondled him, and tantalized him until he came.

The siren of an ambulance woke him in the morning. He crawled out of bed; had to pee so bad it hurt. He stepped over the book of poetry which had fallen off the bed. In the bathroom, he stood at the toilet—his mind blurred. He was disoriented and hung over.

The sound of the phone ringing from the bedroom reverberated in his head like cannon fire. With calculated movements he answered it.

"Hello?" his voice croaked.

"Elliott, this is Allen Dakota. I'm calling to inform you that your leave of absence time is due to run out and you need to return to work. The lab can't carry you any longer."

Elliott scoffed at Dakota's statement. "Do you really think I care about your fucking lab?"

"I've been patient with you and you've been well paid," his boss lectured, "and this is how you show your appreciation?"

"I don't need the work or your fucking money," Elliott yelled. "I've got more than I can spend. Take your lousy job and shove it up your ass with a Bunsen burner!" He hung up.

"Fuck me? Fuck me? No! Fuck you!" he yelled then reached for the half empty glass of scotch sitting on the night stand and took a long swig.

Tempted by thoughts of cutting, he caught his reflection in the dresser mirror. His hand glided over his receding hairline. That and his blonde eyelashes reminded him of his father. He wasn't sure what he loathed more, his features or that he looked like his old man.

He scratched the scraggly red stubble on his pasty white face. Dark circles under his eyes, made worse by his lack of sleep and overindulgence in scotch, looked like bruises.

The temptation of cutting had passed. He made his way back to the bathroom and with the meticulous precision of a surgeon he shaved and rinsed the blade with respectful attention.

The burning pain in his stomach reminded him that he needed to eat.

In the kitchen, he put peanut butter on a stale piece of bread and reached for the carton of milk. Chunky curds filled the glass. He dumped it into the sink and washed his breakfast down with water.

He stood naked in front of the TV and turned it on. ". . . In sports last night, the Tampa Bay Rays swept the New York Yankees in a pre-season game. Carlos Pena's grand slam . . ." He turned it off.

He had his own grand slam at Tropicana Field thanks to Lenny Chambers.

CHAPTER SEVENTY

He wanted so badly to share their lives together that he drove to Anne's building and waited for her to come out.

"See how nice it can be when we spend time together?" he said, watching Anne leave her apartment.

He followed her at a short distance until they reached the shopping center where he parked inconspicuously among other vehicles. He was getting better at this game of Hide and Seek.

"Fuck! Where'd she go . . . oh, the drugstore," and he followed her inside. Hidden behind a rack of tee shirts, he had the perfect vantage point. She picked up a box of tampons.

"Oh Anne," he said under his breath, "I finally understand why you're so moody."

He waited until Anne left the store before he darted to his car. They were driving together like other happy couples.

People went in and out of her office building. A florist van pulled up to the front door and the driver carried in flowers with 'I Love You' balloons.

"For your sake, they'd better not be for you. I am your only love."

An old man wearing coke bottle glasses and a fedora stopped to allow his Jack Russell terrier to sniff the ground near the driver door of the black Toyota. The hyper dog tugged at the leash and began to bark.

"What are you carrying on about, Jackie?" The man bent down to pick up the dog.

Taken aback by the guy gawking at him from the sidewalk, Elliott snapped, "What the fuck you looking at?"

The elder man huffed and walked away with Jackie held tight to his chest. Elliott wouldn't leave until both of them were at the end of the block.

Comfortable that the old fart and the yapping dog were not coming back, Elliott ripped a small piece of duct tape off the roll that be brought from home, got out of his vehicle, and strolled over to the rear of Anne's car. With his free hand, he wiped across the plastic tail light and pressed the tape firmly against the bottom of the fixture.

He hated to leave her but had important errands to run. They would have plenty of time together soon.

Elliott left the liquor store with bottles of champagne and scotch and secured the bags in the trunk. A disturbance in the alley caught his attention. A tall muscle-bound man wearing a sleeveless t-shirt and oversized shorts hanging down below his ass, pulled his fist back and released.

A woman's cry came from the alley.

"I'm gonna kill you, whore!" his fist raised up again to strike.

The cold metal tool cracked across the man's back. He dropped to the ground in a limp heap.

Elliott returned the Karmic tool to its place and drove off.

CHAPTER SEVENTY-ONE

As she walked through the mall, Allison watched the children skate on the indoor ice rink. Parents beamed with pride at their future Olympians, some gliding by, others twirling on the ice.

At the entrance to Macy's, she spotted the Godiva Chocolate counter. Tonight Emma was cooking Chicken Paprikash , Mom's recipe. Allison would bring dessert; chocolate covered cherries. After her candy purchase, she made a bee line for the fifty percent off sale in the shoe department.

#

The Starbucks kiosk was situated next to the skating rink. Elliott ordered a double shot of espresso to ease his lingering hangover. Next stop, Macy's.

Catching his reflection in the store window, he smoothed his hair down and tucked in his shirt; not much he could do about the bags under his eyes.

The blue-haired, pear-shaped, saleslady at the Godiva Chocolate counter who apparently had sampled way too many of her wares, smiled when he approached.

"May I help you?"

He told her that he wanted the largest box of chocolates they had.

"That would be our three hundred dollar box, Sir." She eyed him up and down with discerning scrutiny. "But, we also have lovely boxes for a hundred dollars."

"No, I'll take the big one." He paid with cash and boasted, "That's not too much for the woman I love."

"How sweet." As the woman handed him the box of chocolates, "Your wife will be very happy with these."

"She's not my wife yet, but I'm going to ask her today."

"When you give her this, she'll say yes, for sure!" She flashed him a toothy smile. "I hope she realizes what a lucky gal she is. You're so thoughtful."

He turned and strutted away carrying the red and white package through the store.

#

An elderly lady waylaid Allison as she was about to leave the shoe department with her purchase.

"Oh my goodness," she said taking hold of Allison's forearm, "aren't you the lady who did that psychic show? You're so much prettier in person."

"That's so nice of you to say." Allison patted the woman's hand. Her attention was abruptly drawn toward the door. A man with a red box tucked under his arm approached the exit. A cold shiver coursed through her. She knew there was a connection with Anne Preston, but unclear of the link, she sensed Anne was in danger.

"Please excuse me," Allison backed away, "but I'm in a bit of a hurry."

The arduous fan tightened her hold on Allison's arm. "Gosh, I loved to see you show up those weirdos. You know, I went to a reader once and she told me all about my future. Of course, not much of it came true! My husband Arnold, may he rest in peace, said it was such a waste of money. He died a year ago. Oh, but you probably already know that."

"I'm sorry for your loss," Allison said, gently breaking the hold the woman had on her arm. "It's been nice talking to you but I must run."

"Please if I may," she handed Allison a pen and a sales associate's card from the counter, "could I have your autograph?" The woman scurried away happy with her trophy.

Allison left by the exit where she had last seen the man, not sure of what she would do if she ran into him. Allison stood outside the mall entrance but saw no sign of the man with the red box. She took one last look and turned to leave. Just as it had happened at the crime scenes, she heard 'Karma' and knew what it meant.

"My God, did I just see H.O.K.?"

Despite her determination to mind her own business and to say nothing of Anne's last rebuff, she was compelled to call her. Anne's mailbox was full.

#

Elliott placed his prized package on the table by the front door and opened every window blind. The atmosphere needed to match his exuberant mood. Dust motes danced across beams of sunlight in the unkempt room.

"Note to self," he said, "clean house before you bring home your bride."

He showered again, put on a clean long-sleeved shirt, and buttoned it at the neck and wrists. He opened an unused bottle of aftershave someone at the dental lab had given him at the only Christmas party he ever attended several years ago. Splashing it on his freshly shaved face, the sting on his skin was stimulating.

Tucked away in the back of the dresser drawer was the diamond ring that once belonged to his mother. He held it up to the light, nodded with approval, and replaced it in the black velvet box.

Ready to go—but first, a note to his parents.

Dear Mom and Dad,
I am in love and today I am asking her to marry
me! This is the best day of my life! Even you
can't ruin it.

Your Joyful Son, E

#

A neighbor called a cheerful hello as Allison pulled up to the house. She hurried inside with just a wave and went straight to her office to retrieve the pouch containing the Jewish Star left for her at the library.

She held the object to psychometrize. Nothing new came to her. She laid it on the desk and picked up the pouch. No matter how she concentrated, all she could see was Anne's face.

Anne, you're an idiot! You're protecting him. But he's coming after you because you can identify him.

Again she tried to call Anne. Voicemail full.

Allison shook her head at the perversity of fate.

#

All was in order. For this special occasion, he would drive the convertible. He placed the box on the front seat and smiled into the rearview mirror to check his teeth. He had to be perfect today!

A sudden epiphany, it was Anne, not the karmic deeds he carried out, not the stones, but she, the other half of his soul, who would bring him everlasting happiness.

Confident this feeling would last forever, he left for Anne's office, singing, "I feel good, dada, dada, dada, da."

Before he went in, he combed his wind-blown hair, checked his smile one more time and tossed a mint into his mouth. His breath had to be as sweet as his words. Anticipating their first kiss, he waited for a few minutes to gather up the nerve to propose 'just the right way.'

Making sure he had the ring, he patted his shirt pocket, rehearsed a couple more times, and nervously walked into the building.

Her waiting room was empty. *A good sign.*

He tiptoed to her private office, smiling with anticipation, and leaned forward, ear to the door.

She's talking to someone. FUCK! This'll ruin everything!

Motionless he waited. When he heard her say goodbye and hang up his angst evaporated. She's alone. *Another good sign.*

A gentle tap on the door brought her to him. He got down on one knee and held out the box of chocolates. There she stood.

"Anne, I love you. Will you marry—"

"You're pathetic," and slammed the door in his face. The box crashed to the floor and candies flew all over the carpet. The lock clicked.

Dumbfounded, he called to her through the closed door. "Anne, my love!" He pounded the door with his fists. "Please open up. How could you say that?"

"I told you, Elliott you wanker, leave and don't ever come back!"

Her words burned like battery acid—eating through to his very soul.

"But, I wanted to surprise you. You can't mean what you said."

"The only thing I want is for you to get the hell out of here! You disgust me!"

He scooped up a handful of chocolates from the floor, "You can't cheat Karma!" and squeezed them in his fist.

"You bloody lunatic. I've called the police," she shouted. "They'll be here straightaway."

With the heel of his shoe, he ground spilled candy into the carpet and ran outside to escape the agony; bolted straight to her car; and broke off the windshield wipers. His other hand full of chocolates, he smeared her windshield. The rest of the gooey mess was jammed into the key hole. Enraged, he kicked and dented the door and broke off the side mirror.

He caught the silhouette of Anne standing at her window. She had seen it all. In complete humiliation, he wanted to disappear. The pain he felt was worse than any inflicted on him by his father.

Inside his car, "You ruined everything; you ruined everything; YOU RUINED EVERYTHING!" he screamed until he choked.

#

Anne watched from the window. "Having a tantrum?" she sneered. "Don't think you can intimidate me." She saw him kick the driver side door. "Perhaps I should have called the police!"

Rather, she called the leasing company.

"This is Anne Preston. I've had a bit of trouble at my office. Someone's vandalized my car."

"How bad is it?"

"So bad that I don't intend to drive it!"

"But is it drivable?" He waited. "Ms. Preston, are you there?" He waited.

"It's drivable."

"Should I assume you'd like us to deliver a loaner to your office?"

"Yes, thank you. Can you send the same model and color if you have it, and deliver it to me by six?"

The customer service agent made the arrangements for her loaner then asked whether she'd filed a police report.

"Of course," she told him. "I will give the case number to the driver when he brings the replacement and he'd best bring a roll of paper towels and Windex."

It would take at least an hour before he would get there. Anne ran across the street to the coffee shop, got a take-out latte and headed-back to her office. Her car was visible from the sidewalk. "At least no one witnessed the buffoon having his fit."

She closed up for the day and added the cash receipts to the sizeable bundles in the safe. "Not bad," giving herself a little pat on the back.

The driver called to tell her he had arrived and would wait for her downstairs. Before she went to meet him, she made a quick detour to the janitor's closet where she confiscated a roll of duct tape.

Outside, the young man leaned against the replacement car and stood straight when she approached.

Anne did an inspection. "This car smells like someone was smoking. I don't like driving a car that smells like a tobacco factory."

The young man's face flushed as he stuffed a pack of Camels deeper into his shirt pocket.

"Uh, really? Guess it's better than driving this chocolate-covered Beemer." He turned to the task at hand and wiped the gooey mess off the windshield. "Oh, man! Somebody really did a number on this."

"Yes, they did." She stood cross-armed. "It was probably an arrogant adolescent whom, I might add, most likely smokes!"

Bits of chocolate stained the paperwork he handed to Anne. "The boss said to pick up the Police Report."

"That won't be necessary," Anne quipped. "I faxed it to him before I came down."

He seemed unsure.

"Do you doubt me? Shall I ring up your boss? I wanted to have a word with him regarding the smoke in the car anyway." Without another word, he handed her the keys and drove away in the damaged vehicle—duct tape partially covered the tail light.

"Elliott, you ignoramus, how clever you must feel."

Anne placed a piece of silver tape on the tail light in the precise location Elliott had positioned it on the other vehicle. She knew she couldn't switch the license plate but hoped Elliott wouldn't notice the new one.

CHAPTER SEVENTY-TWO

Elliott stormed into his bedroom and knocked the 'Anne' pillow off the bed—the effigy he had embraced with the tenderness of a new groom the night before, and dragged it to the kitchen. He repeated her words: pathetic, lunatic. Blinded by rage, he plunged a butcher knife deep into the pillow and ripped it apart. His pain a palpable force.

"Who the FUCK do you think you are?" He stabbed again. "Humiliate me? I'll have you one way or the other!" His anger so intense he didn't feel the knife slice deep into his left hand.

Exhausted, he dropped to the floor and watched the blood puddle. Dipping his right index finger into the crimson pool on the terrazzo floor, he wrote 'Karma.'

Lying next to him on the floor was the torn pillowcase which he used to cover the gaping wound in his hand. Blood still dripped.

A thin morning light filtered through the kitchen window and shined into his eyes. He strained against the cabinet to pull himself off the floor and knocked over a chair. Zombie-like, he trudged to the desk and opened his journal.

Mom, Dad,

There's been a slight change of plans. You'll soon have company.

Your Son, the Schmuck!

CHAPTER SEVENTY-THREE

Outside Allison's window, a blustering wind, which preceded the approaching rain, caused palm branches to brush against the panes of glass. Seated at her desk, Allison daydreamed and saw the reality of her situation—there was no place to turn. Emma would stop her. The police wouldn't listen. Steve, that's a dead-end. She was overwhelmed by frustration.

Before long, fragmented images flashed in her mind; a brick parking garage draped with red, white, and blue banners; a dolphin fountain; Alivia's Boutique.

"Alivia's? That's where I got my black dress. It's in Hyde Park!"

In the midst of analyzing the images, she had a vision of 'Karma' written in blood.

She had no doubt now—it was H.O.K. she saw.

Allison remembered that when she researched Anne for her television show, there was nothing found on her via the internet. Without a home address or land line number, she had no choice but to go to her office.

She left early in the morning for Anne's office. On her way, Allison skirted around palm fronds that littered the streets from the unrelenting storm last night. Landscapers were cleaning up debris scattered over the parking lot as Allison rushed to the front door of the office building.

She knocked repeatedly on the locked door to Anne's office. No response. Allison scribbled a note and ripped the page out of her spiral notebook then slipped it under the door.

#

Anne picked up the note and read:

> *Anne,*
> *I've been trying to reach you. It's imperative that you contact me. 727-555-1284.*
> *Allison Rogers*

"My, you are persistent, Allison Rogers." She fed the note into the shredder then turned back to double check what she had done. Every last scrap of paper was shredded, even the empty pages from her Day Planner.

She walked over to the window, pulled the louvers aside, and monitored Allison as she made her way to her car.

Convinced the determined pest had gone, Anne returned to the job at hand. She wrapped the Baccarat crystal paperweight in tissue paper and placed it in a small box.

Her last act was to open the safe and empty her stash into her briefcase.

CHAPTER SEVENTY-FOUR

The quaint Florida town of Dunedin is the sister city to Dunedin, Scotland. On this warm Florida afternoon, Elliott was momentarily distracted from the dull throb in his hand by the performers of the Bagpipe Festival taking place on Main Street.

He popped a couple of aspirin in his mouth and chewed. He crossed the street after the marchers passed by and entered the upscale shop.

With fastidious care, he selected new bed linens and lavender spray. Elliott left the store and walked out to the busy sidewalk. He stopped at a vendor and bought a bag of shortbread cookies which he ate along with more aspirin.

He returned home with several shopping bags and an unrelenting ache in his hand; the pain now moving up his arm.

He deposited the packages on the kitchen table. 'Karma,' written on the floor in blood, reminded him of what needed to be done.

First things first; he'd make his usual evening drive to her condo to check that Anne's car was there. He'd stay long enough to make sure that she was in for the night. Then he could sleep.

The slash in his hand was infected; it was red and swollen, and he had a fever. He found old pain pills in the back of the medicine cabinet, left over from root canal surgery several years ago, and washed them down with two gulps of scotch.

He also found half a bottle of erythromycin tablets and washed some of them down, too.

Slowed down by his injury and the combination of alcohol and pain pills, it took a full day to scrub, polish and set up their matrimonial suite. He made sure to take frequent breaks from his work to re-bandage his swollen and oozing hand. It would be sacrilegious to defile the purity of this room with any foulness from his wound.

Plagued by nausea and clutching bursts of pain, he forced himself to stay focused. He stapled news clippings of all of his victims on the bedroom walls in chronological order so she could see the totality of his accomplishments. Satisfied with his efforts, he stepped back and admired his work.

Candles were placed just so for the proper light; lavender water was sprayed on the new pillows and sheets. And, at the foot of the bed, he laid out the modest white nightgown for her to wear.

"I'm doing this for us, Anne. Once I bring you home, our lives will be perfect."

He made a quick trip to his car. The chilled night air in the garage felt good against his naked body, sweaty with fever.

After he removed a sleeping bag from the storage closet and placed it in the trunk of the Toyota along with the new blanket he had purchased in Dunedin, he opened his work bag and slipped the hunting knife out of its leather sheath.

In the kitchen, he spent an hour rubbing a wet stone against the blade then polished the knife until it glistened. He laid it next to the book of poetry on the nightstand on his side of the bed and covered it with a white lace handkerchief.

"It won't hurt at all."

Worn out and weak from the infection that had started to take its toll, he needed to rest. He stretched out on the sofa and closed his eyes. Sleep lasted for an hour or two and then he'd wake with chills.

The sound of the trash truck woke him. Still groggy and achy, he had to make it to her apartment before she left!

He threw on yesterday's clothes, snatched his keys, ran to the garage and raced to her building. She pulled out onto the road just as he arrived. Surprised to see that her car had been repaired so quickly, he was relieved that the tape on the tail light was still in place.

A good sign.

It was the beginning of President's Day weekend, traffic was light, but adequate cars to keep him concealed. He maneuvered behind a red Jeep and remained in position.

Anne drove past her office building and continued driving over the causeway to Tampa.

The Jeep he trailed turned at an intersection. He slowed and allowed the car behind him to pass. He sped up and took his place behind it and continued this tactic until her car turned off onto a side street and pulled into the red brick parking garage in Hyde Park. He waited a couple of minutes before driving in.

He inched his car up the ramp, level by level, his eyes searched for her. When he hadn't spotted her on Level 6, he parked and walked up the ramp hiding himself behind the concrete supports.

She was parked on the deck above, talking to a man who was removing a helmet from a motorcycle.

Inflamed by jealousy, he took a step forward, then halted when he saw the man point, as if giving her directions. The cyclist mounted his bike and left.

Elliott moved aside when the Harley drove past.

Anne entered the stairwell.

He hurried to the elevator, reached the ground floor and waited. He watched her from a doorway until he saw her walk across the street. She stopped in front of the window of Alivia's Boutique, adjusted her jacket and entered.

#

Anne casually browsed up and down the aisles and tried on designer clothes she knew she wouldn't buy.

"Thank you, ladies," Anne chirped. "I'll be back next week when your new line arrives."

#

Elliott stepped out of the shadows and into the bright sunlight, pulling his baseball cap down low. He followed her to another shop and waited. She came out of the Louis Vuitton store carrying a brown shopping bag.

#

Seated under a red and white striped umbrella on the patio of Café Bella, Anne placed her package on the empty chair next to her. She opened the bag and admired her new tote.

Comfortable in the shade beneath the colorful canvas, she watched passers-by and leisurely sipped on a glass of wine and ate her Cobb Salad.

#

At a gas station across the street, he ate a dried-up candy bar from a vending machine and watched her from a vantage point behind the air pump.

The longer he waited in the heat, the more his head pounded and his hand swelled. Pain moved up his arm. Having used the last of the pain pills the day before, he popped a half dozen aspirin into his mouth and chewed. Now his stomach burned; and the dick behind the counter inside spied on him through the window.

#

It was a smug attitude Anne had knowing her Louis Vuitton tote cost more than her foster parents paid for their car. She took the garage elevator to the roof, put her package in the trunk, and drove west over the causeway toward home.

She made it all the way to Clearwater when the traffic slowed to a crawl. Cars jockeyed around for a better position. A quick glance in the side mirror showed her traffic was backed up as far as she could see.

A news helicopter passed overhead. Anne turned the volume up on the radio. Minutes later, the report of a jack-knifed tractor trailer on US 60 was announced. "Expect delays of more than an hour . . ."

"Good thing I had an ample lunch."

CHAPTER SEVENTY-FIVE

"Die, asshole!" Elliott laid on the horn and slammed on the brakes. He cut the wheel and accelerated into a gap in traffic and glared at the driver as he passed the RV towing a Smart Car. With three cars between her BMW and him; he followed her to the beach.

Elliott waited and watched from across the street of her building until ten o'clock. "Goodnight, Anne," he said aloud, and drove off.

The closest gas station on the main road was lit up like broad daylight. He waited until a pick-up truck drove away from the pump then started to move forward. A red Corvette zipped in front of him and took Elliott's spot. The driver remained in his car talking on his cell forcing Elliott to move to an open pump.

On his way inside to pay for his gas, he caught a glimpse of the middle-aged man with a sweater tied around his shoulders get out of the Corvette and place the nozzle in the tank.

Famished and in pain, Elliott stood in line to pay for a couple of sandwiches, water, and a bottle of extra-strength pain relievers. The old man in front of him fumbled to count out change for his cigarettes then dropped the handful of coins on the floor. The flustered old guy apologized and started counting over.

Perspiration beaded on Elliott's forehead. He removed his ball cap and used his sleeve to wipe away the sweat then tugged his hat low and waited for the man to move away from the counter. He reached into his pocket for his wallet when the wanna-be stud from the Corvette butted in line and slapped a five dollar bill on the counter and asked for a couple of Lotto Quick Pics.

He huffed at Elliott, "I'm in a hurry."

Elliott stepped in front of him to cut him off.

"Oh, for Christ's sake," the Vette man complained, "go ahead and buy your stupid shit."

Elliott paid for his purchase, took the stud's money from the counter and threw the wadded bill on the floor before he walked out.

#

"Son of a bitch!" The front windshield of his Corvette was shattered. He crammed the lottery tickets in his pocket and dialed 9-1-1.

"I saw everything!" an excited teenage girl ran up to him waving her phone. "I got a picture of his tag."

#

Elliott made it as far as the driveway when the nausea hit him with a vengeance. He threw the car door open and puked. Stumbling to the house, he braced himself against the threshold with his bad hand. The wound re-opened and bled profusely. He heaved again.

Too tired to undress, he wrapped a dish cloth around his hand, collapsed on the sofa and fell into a coma-like sleep.

#

It was twenty-two seventeen hours when the call was dispatched to Pinellas County Sheriff's Deputy, Ian Webster whose shift had started at twenty-two hundred hours. Harvey Richardson reported that his classic Corvette's windshield had been smashed by 'some druggie scum bag.' Deputy Webster arrived and interviewed the witnesses. Bernice Jones, the girl who snapped a photo of the car tag, was happy to show her handiwork to the deputy. "And I saw him do it!"

He ran the plate through the FCIC/NCIC database. The black 2009 Toyota was registered to an Elliott Seymour Gelman, current address: 277 Pennock Street, Clearwater, Florida 33778. No hits on outstanding warrants or previous arrests.

Deputy Webster called in the report from inside his patrol car. A call came in and he was dispatched to a five car motor vehicle accident with possible fatalities. He'd have to question Elliott Gelman later.

Richardson approached the patrol car. "Are you going to arrest him now?" he demanded.

"Sir, we have to investigate before we can arrest anyone."

"This is going to cost at least fifteen hundred dollars to fix. And, you're not going to do anything about a drugged up maniac running loose?"

"Mr. Richardson, if this guy did it, he'll be arrested and charged with Felony Criminal Mischief. I understand how you must feel. We'll be in touch with you as soon as we complete our investigation." The deputy left with lights and sirens in response to the M.V.A.

#

The pain in his arm woke him before sunrise. Elliott went to the bathroom and unwrapped the bandages from his hand. It had stopped bleeding. He poured a bottle of peroxide over the smelly wound. White foam covered his palm. He re-wrapped his hand and was astonished at how much better it felt.

There wasn't a chance in hell that he'd be late again. The early morning sun was a red fireball on the horizon when he arrived at Anne's apartment building. Her car was still parked in the same place but there was no sign of her.

Noon came and went. No Anne.

He was hot and drank the last of the water he had, washing down more aspirin. Now he had to take a leak. He couldn't leave so he pissed into one of the empty water bottles, opened the door, and rolled it under the car.

Dinner time: still no Anne. "Where the fuck is she?"

To avoid being harassed by another curious cop, he moved his car a half a block away.

There she is! It was worth the wait. She was a beauty; her red hair caught in a puff of evening breeze.

"She's wearing pants that show off her tush just for me. What now?" he mumbled. She disappeared into the building, then returned with a package and placed it in the trunk of her car.

#

The motor vehicle accident had Deputy Webster tied up for the entire shift the night before last and he couldn't continue the investigation of the Gelman case. He made it his priority at the start of his shift to drive to the Gelman residence to follow-up on the Richardson complaint.

The Deputy arrived at 277 Pennock Street and detected vomit on the driveway and what appeared to be blood smeared on the frame of the front door. He knocked several times and identified himself. There was no response. He had a bad feeling—he'd better call it in.

"Sarge, I might have a situation here. There are signs of vomit and blood at the entrance to this residence. I'm going to check around the property."

At six foot three inches tall, Deputy Webster could easily see through the window into the kitchen where there appeared to have been a struggle. A pool of blood, some bloody rags and a butcher knife were on the floor.

He radioed for backup. "Sarge, I need a supervisor here . . ."

A call went out over the radio to the Fire Department to remove the door and for medics to be on scene.

Neighbors, some still in their bathrobes, gathered outside to see the cause of the commotion.

The door to the house was removed. Paramedics and Fire Department personnel waited outside while Deputy Webster and his sergeant entered the property. They checked room by room for a victim. What they saw on the bedroom walls gave them cause to call for detectives.

CHAPTER SEVENTY-SIX

Emma poked her nose into Allison's room. "It's two o'clock in the afternoon. What are you doing in your pj's?"

"Just catching up on paperwork." She wished she could tell her sister of her frustration with Anne Preston, of her concerns about H.O.K., and that she was on edge and anxious.

"This is the last day of the President's Day Weekend sale," Emma coaxed. "Shoes are fifty percent off at Macy's. Want to join me?"

President's Day banners. Hyde Park. He's there today! "Sorry, Em, I'm up to my ears with work. I'll see you when you get back."

The garage door closed. Emma left. Allison dressed, picked up her digital camera and keys, and drove to Hyde Park. "Forget Anne. It's H.O.K. I need to find." All she'd have to do is take a picture of him and get his license number. She wouldn't let him slip away again. Sergeant Vernon would have to do something.

#

Anne drove onto the road. Elliott followed keeping his distance.

He wiped the sweat from his eyes; his clothes were soaked; his teeth chattered. He turned the heater on full blast!

A horn honked. He stepped on the gas.

She was just ahead. He had no problem sticking close until they reached the light at the Feather Sound industrial park.

"FUCK!"

She drove through the intersection just as the signal turned red. He had to stop. A fucking cop car was across the street.

Sweat rolled down the back of his neck but he was cold.

Green light!

"Where are you?" His eyes strained to see further ahead.

"Get the fuck out of my way!" he shouted to the driver in front of him. He followed inches away from the vehicle. The driver shot him the finger.

"You're lucky. Another time and I'd snap that finger off!"

He saw her! The tape on the tail light really worked. "Just call me James Fuckin' Bond." He followed her all the way to Hyde Park.

She made her routine turn into the parking garage.

Elliott continued past the entrance, making a U-turn and entered the garage only after he felt certain she had time to park on her usual level at the top.

The garage was practically empty with most offices closed for the holiday. He had his sign! He'd have to be careful; every noise made an echo.

He parked on the fifth level next to the stairwell door. It would be easier to put her in the trunk from here. He opened the driver-side door.

DING. DING. DING.

"FUCK!" He jerked the key from the ignition and held his breath. *Did she hear that?* He pressed the release button for the trunk and slithered out of the car like a snake in the grass, crouching between the car and the wall.

With the lid raised he reached in for the tire iron, placed it at his feet, then unrolled the sleeping bag and put the soft fluffy blanket on top.

She wouldn't know the care he'd given to prepare her bed for the short ride home. No matter. He knew.

He lowered the trunk lid but not all the way. It'd be easy to lift with her in his arms.

With the cool metal rod tucked under his arm, he stepped to the stairwell door and pulled. It opened easily, making a slight *click* when it closed. Once the door was secured behind him, he reached up, shielded his eyes, and holding the tire iron, struck the overhead light fixture one time. A shower of glass fell at his feet with surprisingly little noise. He waited for any response to the breaking bulb. Silence.

He propped the door ajar with the tool and climbed the first set of steps, crossed the landing, turned, and continued up the second set of stairs to the sixth floor and halted.

He cracked the heavy metal door open a little and leaned in to hear better.

A car door slammed. An engine started.

Tires screeched as they descended the ramp.

"FUCK! She's leaving!"

Panicked, he opened the door wider in time to see an SUV driven by a woman wearing a red hat, pass by him.

Relieved that his plan was still viable, he sneaked out from his hiding place, rushed to the ramp and saw Anne above walking toward the stairwell, a brown satchel in hand.

He bounded for the door, yanked it open and tripped—his fall stopped when he grabbed the stair rail with his injured hand. Bile backed up in his mouth from the pain when the infected gash split open. He collapsed to his knees. A gasp filled his lungs. He forced himself to exhale and stumbled on the landing, then continued his flight down, barely able to breathe through the excruciating pain.

He slowed, rounded the corner and made his way to the fifth floor where the door had been propped open by the tire iron. He steeled himself, found his spot around the bend on the landing, now camouflaged by the darkness from the broken light. His back pressed tight to the wall. He was invisible.

The door above opened.

She's coming to me!

The bandage on his wound was soaked, his hand useless. With his right hand, he reached into his shirt pocket and pulled out the plastic bag with the chloroform-soaked rag. He held his breath and used his teeth to hold the Baggie so he could pull it open and remove the damp cloth.

He was ready.

The echo of her shoes on the concrete steps came to a halt. He strained to hear. Seconds seemed like minutes.

Did she forget something? His heart beat pounded so loud in his ears he was afraid she might hear it.

She stepped onto his landing and surrounded by darkness, walked right past him.

From the shadows behind her, he lunged—the rag raised to cover her face.

She thrust her elbow back into his ribs and knocked him off balance.

He staggered back, slipped on a piece of broken glass from the light, and slammed into the wall.

The chloroformed rag dropped from his hand.

It took a nanosecond for her to turn and face him. His alarm turned to horror when he saw a laser beam aimed at his chest.

She fired.

He dropped to the ground, paralyzed. Two darts attached to wires stuck out of his chest. He was unable to make a sound.

#

She only had thirty seconds before he would come out of it. "Twenty-nine, twenty-eight, twenty-seven" she counted aloud, and tossed the taser gun next to him; wires remained connected to the cartridge. She didn't worry about the serial numbers, the taser was registered to Anna Goldberg in Washington State.

With her gloved hands, she reached into her tote bag.

"Twenty-four, twenty-three, twenty-two."

She removed a full container of kerosene along with the newspaper page showing a photo of Jennifer Barrett.

"Fourteen, thirteen, twelve."

His eyes were squeezed shut; his mouth in a tight grimace.

She doused his body with kerosene and tossed the container next to his head.

"Seven, six, five."

She saw the tire iron that propped open the door, gripped it with both hands and without hesitation: THWACK! It landed across the bridge of his nose. She dropped the tool on his body.

"Now this is Karma!"

She lit the newspaper and tossed it on the saturated heap that was Elliott Gelman.

WHOOSH!

Anne picked up her bag and watched from the doorway until flames and smoke drove her from the landing.

"I told you, you don't know me!"

#

Ten minutes away. Allison sensed he was already there. She had to hurry.

SIRENS!

"Oh, crap! Not now." A speeding ticket was the last thing she needed at this moment. Blue and red lights flashed in the rearview mirror. Allison pulled off to the right. The police car sped past.

Emergency vehicles and police cars lined the streets around the parking garage she had so clearly seen in her vision. Allison struggled through the crowd that had formed on the sidewalks and made her way to the police barriers.

"Excuse me, Sir?" Allison called to a deputy passing nearby. "What happened?"

"Fire in the stairwell," he said, and continued walking away. He yelled to another officer, "Get these people back!"

She moved through the crowd searching for Anne certain she would spot her red hair. She couldn't identify H.O.K. but she believed they'd be together. Allison fought her way through the pack, but her effort to find Anne was futile.

Anonymous voices murmured from the onlookers.

"Probably smartass kids setting a trash can on fire."

"Hey! Why's Channel Six here for a trash fire?"

"I heard they found a body inside. Burned to a crisp."

Looky-loos pressed in closer to the barricades as the coroner's van edged its way into the structure. An odd mixture of emotions overpowered Allison when it drove by—relief, conclusion, and liberation. There was no point in her staying. The prepossessing threat of the Stone Killer was gone. She knew she was free of her connection to Anne Preston and to H.O.K., but whose body was found in the stairwell?

Allison stashed her camera into the glove box of her car. Another news van approached as she drove away.

#

A fisherman preparing to launch his boat into Tampa Bay was shocked to find a submerged car near the boat ramp. It appeared from the skid marks in the sand that the vehicle veered off the highway and plunged into the bay.

Police were called to the scene and the BMW was removed from the water. Windows were open; headlights on; gear positioned in Drive; keys in the ignition. There was no one inside. A small red purse was discovered in the car along with a suitcase filled with women's clothes. Identification found in the handbag was that of Anne Preston of Clearwater Beach, Florida.

After a search was completed by the Tampa Police dive team, no body was discovered. The investigation was turned over to Tampa Police detectives.

CHAPTER SEVENTY-SEVEN

The early morning sun reflected off the water of Allen's Creek. Although the weather on the west coast of Florida was often unpredictable in the month of March, on this day it was perfect. A manatee rolled in the water just beyond the dock. Its calf stayed close to its momma.

The arrival of spring brought the end of a long, dark year for Allison and the promise of new beginnings.

She read aloud to Emma from the article in the <u>Tampa Courier</u>.

". . . The Medical Examiner's report has positively determined the identity of the charred body discovered in the Hyde Park garage on February twentieth as that of forty-year-old Elliott Gelman of Clearwater.

Sergeant Geoff Vernon of the Pinellas County Sheriff's Office said, 'We have reason to believe that evidence found in Gelman's home will tie him to a number of unsolved homicides in the State of Florida.'

Gelman had worked as a dental ceramist in St. Petersburg. His former boss, Alan Dakota said, "He was a great guy and an excellent employee. We were shocked to hear what happened to him."

Allison frowned, wadded the newspaper and tucked it under her chair.

"I know what that face means," Emma declared. "Why don't I

go in and make a pitcher of Mimosas?" Emma had only been gone a minute when she returned.

"Guess who I found ringing the doorbell, Allison!" Emma held the crook of Steve's arm and led him to the dock.

"Steve?" Allison remained seated and put on her sunglasses to hide her un-mascara'd eyelashes.

"I brought you a peace offering; Opening Day tickets for the Rays, right behind home plate." He handed them to her. "I was hoping we could start over."

He was so easy to read. Allison felt a pang of desire that she knew he felt as well.

"Steve, you may be easy to resist, but those tickets are not, so I suppose it's a date." Allison reached out to shake on it.

"This would be a good time for me to go back in and make those Mimosas," Emma grinned all the way to the kitchen.

Water splashed. "Are those manatees I see?" Steve watched them frolic until they disappeared under the water. He sat next to Allison and noticed the crumpled newspaper. "I can assume you've read the article. It wasn't exactly the six lottery numbers, but it was damn close!"

"I'll take that as a compliment . . . and an apology." She looked into his smiling blue eyes and knew that this was the start of something wonderful.

EPILOGUE

It had been a whirlwind year. Philadelphia was the last stop on her three-month book tour and Allison was happy to be heading home. She settled into the comfortable leather seat, grateful that her plane would depart on time.

The passenger across the aisle was reading Allison's book, Psychic Awareness. She smiled to herself and thought about the many changes that took place in her life after the death of the Stone Killer; her book making the <u>New York Times</u> Bestsellers List, personal appearances, the movie option.

What she wanted most was to see Steve. She missed him so much. Allison glanced down at her engagement ring and smiled remembering the night at Maggiano's, their now favorite restaurant, how Steve got down on bended knee to propose as the violinist played <u>Take Me Out To The Ballgame</u>.

#

Emma had done a great job of coordinating the final wedding plans in Allison's absence as well as organizing her fan mail while she was traveling. Allison stepped into her office and was flabbergasted at the amount of mail that had accumulated over the last couple of weeks. If this volume kept up, she'd have to hire a secretary. In the meantime, she'd get through it little by little.

Emma entered the room carrying a handful of letters and a small package.

"This just came for you," she said, placing the mail on the desk and handing the box to Allison.

There was no return address, just the postmark from Philadelphia.

Inside the box, wrapped in layers of tissue, was the Baccarat crystal paperweight along with a note.

Check Mate.

ABOUT THE AUTHORS

Judith Haimes worked with law enforcement as a consultant. She is member of the National Society of Arts and Letters, and the national writer's organization—Sisters in Crime. She was a syndicated columnist and is the subject of the book, Judith. She resides in Clearwater, Florida with her husband.

NanC Hensley is a member of Sisters in Crime—a national writer's organization, worked as a consultant with law enforcement, and has been a Clinical Hypnotherapist since 1992. She has published numerous articles on the topic of metaphysics. She currently lives in Pinellas County, Florida.